"I am Theo Markou Garcia," he said in the way men did when they expected to be known, recognized. Celebrated.

"I'm Becca, the bastard daughter of the sister no one dares mention out loud."

"I know who you are." This time, it was his low, insinuating voice that seemed to reverberate behind her ribs, and spread out through her bones. "As for what I want, I don't think that's the right question."

"It's the right question if you want me to whirl around in front of you," Becca countered, some recklessness charging through her, making her courageous. "Though I doubt you'll give me the right answer."

"The right question is this—what do you want, and how can I give it to you? And then the only other question is, how far are you willing to go to get what you want?"

All about the author…
Caitlin Crews

CAITLIN CREWS discovered her first romance novel at the age of twelve. It involved swashbuckling pirates, grand adventures, a heroine with rustling skirts and a mind of her own, and a seriously mouthwatering and masterful hero. The book (the title of which remains lost in the mists of time) made a serious impression. Caitlin was immediately smitten with romances and romance heroes, to the detriment of her middle school social life. And so began her lifelong love affair with romance novels, many of which she insists on keeping near her at all times.

Caitlin has made her home in places as far-flung as York, England, and Atlanta, Georgia. She was raised near New York City, and fell in love with London on her first visit when she was a teenager. She has backpacked in Zimbabwe, been on safari in Botswana and visited tiny villages in Namibia. She has, while visiting the place in question, declared her intention to live in Prague, Dublin, Paris, Athens, Nice, the Greek Islands, Rome, Venice and/or any of the Hawaiian islands. Writing about exotic places seems like the next best thing to moving there.

She currently lives in California, with her animator/comic book artist husband and their menagerie of ridiculous animals.

Other titles by Caitlin Crews available in ebook

Harlequin Presents®

Caitlin Crews

THE REPLACEMENT WIFE

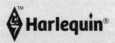

TORONTO NEW YORK LONDON
AMSTERDAM PARIS SYDNEY HAMBURG
STOCKHOLM ATHENS TOKYO MILAN MADRID
PRAGUE WARSAW BUDAPEST AUCKLAND

Recycling programs
for this product may
not exist in your area.

ISBN-13: 978-0-373-13076-4

THE REPLACEMENT WIFE

First North American publication 2012

THE REPLACEMENT WIFE

To Kate Rogers for her unsung, invaluable help before, and to Megan Bassett, my editor, for making all my books so very much better.

CHAPTER ONE

THE HOUSE HAD not improved since she'd seen it last. It loomed over New York City's tony Fifth Avenue like a displeased society matron, all disapproving elegance and a style that dated to the excesses of the Gilded Age. Becca Whitney sat in the vast and chilly parlor, stuffed with priceless paintings and fussy, disturbingly detailed statuary, and tried to pretend she couldn't feel the way her two so-called relatives were glaring at her. As if her presence there, as the illegitimate daughter of their disinherited and long-disparaged late sister, polluted the very air.

Maybe it did, Becca thought. Maybe that was one reason the great hulking mansion felt like a soulless crypt.

The strained silence—that Becca refused to break, since she'd been called here this time and was thankfully no longer the supplicant—was broken suddenly, by the slight creaking sound of the ornate parlor door.

Thank God, Becca thought. She had to keep her hands tightly laced together in her lap, her teeth clenched in her jaw, to keep the bitter words she'd *like* to say from spilling out. Whatever this interruption was, it was a relief.

Until she looked up and saw the man who stepped

inside the room. Something like warning, like anticipation, seemed to crackle over her skin, making it hum in reaction. Making her sit straighter in her chair.

"Is this the girl?" he asked, his voice a low, dark rumble, his tone brisk. Demanding.

Everything—power, focus, the strained air itself—shifted immediately. Away from the horrible aunt and uncle she'd never planned to see again and toward the man, dark and big and goose bump-raising, who moved as if he expected the world to shuffle and rearrange itself around him—and with the kind of confidence that suggested it usually did exactly that.

Becca felt her lips part slightly as their eyes met, across centuries of artifacts and the frowns of these terrible people who had tossed her mother out like so much trash twenty-six years ago. His were a rich, arresting color, an electric amber, and seared into her, making her blink. Making her wonder if she'd been scarred by the contact.

Who was he?

He was not particularly tall, not much over six feet, but he was…*there*. A force to be reckoned with, as if a live wire burned in him, and from him. He wore the same kind of clothes they all wore in this hermetically sealed world of wealth and privilege—expensive. Yet unlike her fussy relatives, in their suits and scarves and ostentatious accessories, everything about this man was stripped down. Lean. Powerful. Impressive. A charcoal-gray sweater that clung to his perfectly shaped torso, and dark trousers that outlined the strength of his thighs and his narrow hips. He looked elegant and elemental all at once.

He gazed at her, his head cocking slightly to one side as he considered her, and Becca knew two things with every cell in her body. The first was that he was dangerous in a way she could not quite grasp—though she could see the fierce intelligence in him, coupled with a certain ruthless intensity. And the second was that she had to get away from him. *Now.* Her stomach cramped and her heart pounded. Something about him just…spooked her.

"You see it, then," Becca's pompous uncle Bradford said in the same patronizing tone he'd used when he'd thrown Becca out of this very same house six months ago. In the very same tone he'd used to tell her that she and her sister Emily were mistakes. Embarrassments. Certainly not Whitneys. "The resemblance."

"It is uncanny." The man's remarkable, disconcerting eyes narrowed, focused entirely on Becca even as he spoke to her uncle. "I thought you exaggerated."

Becca stared back at him. Something was alive, hot, in the air between them. She felt her mouth dry, her palms twitch. *Panic,* she thought. It was only panic, and perfectly reasonable! She wanted to leap to her feet and run out into the streets, far away from this overwrought place and the scene unfolding around her that she no longer wanted to understand—but she couldn't seem to move. It was the way he looked at her. The command in it, perhaps. The heat. It kept her still. Obedient.

"I still don't know why I'm here," Becca said, forcing herself to speak. To do something other than mutely obey. She turned and looked at Bradford, and her mother's pursed-mouthed sister, the censorious Helen. "After the way you threw me out the last time—"

"This has nothing to do with that," her uncle—a technical title at best, in Becca's opinion—sniffed impatiently. "This is important."

"So is my sister's education," Becca replied, a snap

in her voice. She was too aware of the other man, like a dark shadow in her peripheral vision. She could feel the way his eyes ate her up, consumed her. It made her lungs feel tight in her chest. It made her body…*ache*.

"For God's sake, Bradford," Helen murmured to her brother, twisting the elegant rings on her fingers. "What can you be thinking? *Look* at this creature. *Listen* to her! Who would ever believe that she was one of us?"

"*She* has about as much interest in being 'one of you' as she does in walking back home to Boston naked, over a sea of broken glass," Becca retorted, but then reminded herself to focus on the reason she'd come back here, the reason she'd subjected herself to this. "All I want from you people is what I've always wanted from you. Help with my sister's education. I still don't see how that's too much to ask."

She waved a hand at the immense and obvious wealth all around them, from the thick, soft rugs beneath their feet to the paintings all over the walls, to the graceful ceilings above them, bursting with exquisite chandeliers. To say nothing of the fact that this was a family-owned mansion that took up a full city block in the middle of New York City. Becca did not have to know anything about Manhattan real estate to understand that the family who didn't want to claim her could certainly afford to do so, if they wished, without noticing the difference.

Not that it was Becca who needed them to claim her. It was her seventeen-year-old sister, Emily. Bright, smart, destined-for-great-things Emily, who deserved more than the kind of life Becca could fashion for her on a paralegal's salary. Only Emily's need could ever have inspired Becca to seek out these people and prostate herself before them in the first place. Only Emily's best interests could ever have compelled her to respond to this latest summons after Bradford had called her mother a whore and had Becca removed from these very premises half a year ago. Just as it was only thoughts of the tuition money Emily still desperately needed, now that Becca's savings were depleted, that kept her from making a rude gesture at Bradford as he scowled at her now.

That and the fact she'd made her mother a promise on her deathbed: that she would do whatever she had to do to protect Emily from suffering. Anything at all. And how could she break that promise when her mother had given up this whole, glittering world for Becca years ago?

"Stand up," came the silky demand from beside her—much closer than it should have been. Becca jumped slightly in her seat, and then hated herself for showing that much weakness. Somehow, she knew it would count against her. She turned, and the devil himself was standing too close to her, still looking at her in that disturbing way.

What was it about this man that got under her skin like this? So quickly? So completely? When she didn't even know his name?

"I…what?" she asked, startled.

This close, she could see that, while he could never be called handsome, precisely, the way his features came together—so dark and brooding, with that olive skin and his piercing eyes—made him distractingly compelling in a purely, breathtakingly masculine way. It was as if the very fact of his full lips made something in her *want* to revel in her own femininity, like a cat in a sunbeam.

Where had that thought come from?

"Stand up," he said again, with that note of command ringing in his voice, and she found she was moving without meaning to do so. Drifting up and on to her feet like a marionette in his control. Becca was horrified at herself. It was as if he'd hypnotized her—as if those eyes of his were a snake charmer's, and she was helpless to do anything but dance for his pleasure.

On her feet, she found he was taller than she'd thought, forcing her to tilt her head back slightly to meet his gaze—which she did, even though the wild beat of her pulse wanted her to break and run, to escape, to get far away from him….

"This is fascinating," he murmured. His lean, intriguing face was closer now, and she had the sense of the great control he practiced, the power he kept to himself, the hum and the kick of it, as if he operated on a different frequency than the rest of the world. "Turn."

Becca only stared at him, and so he lifted a hand and twirled a finger in the air, demonstration and command. It was a hard, strong hand. Not soft and pale like her uncle's. It was the hand of a man who was not afraid to use it to do his own work. She had a sudden, stark and erotic vision of that hand against her own skin, and had to swallow against it. Hard.

"I would love nothing more than to obey your every command," she managed to say, shocked at the sudden swell of carnal need that washed through her, and fighting to shove it behind her carefully cultivated tough exterior. "But I don't even know who you are, or what you want, or why you think you have the right to command anyone in the first place."

As if from a distance, she heard her aunt and her uncle let out sharp gasps and exclamations, but Becca couldn't bring herself to care about them. She was mesmerized, spellbound, caught up in the man before her and his searing amber eyes.

How strange that she should find him so unsettling, while at the same time she had the notion that he could keep her safe. Even here. She pushed the absurdity away. *Unlikely,* she thought. *This man is about as safe as broken glass.*

He did not smile. But his gaze warmed, and Becca felt an answering warmth flood her, turning into flame wherever it touched.

"I am Theo Markou Garcia," he said in the way men did when they expected to be known, recognized. Celebrated. When she only stared back at him, his lips curved slightly—almost wryly, she thought. "I am the CEO of Whitney Media."

Whitney Media was the great jewel of the Whitney family—the modern-day reason they still held on to so much of their old robber baron money and were able to maintain latter-day castles like this one. Becca knew very little about the actual company. Except perhaps that through it and because of it, thanks to the newspapers and cable channels and movie studios, the Whitneys owned far too much, had too much influence, and had come to regard themselves as demigods in the way only the very rich could.

"Congratulations," she said dryly. She raised her eyebrows. "I'm Becca, the bastard daughter of the sister no one dares mention out loud." She shot a look toward her aunt and uncle, wishing she could incinerate them with the force of it. "Her name was Caroline, and she was better than the both of you put together."

"I know who you are." This time, it was his low, insinuating voice that blocked out the noise from the other, legitimate, and now further affronted Whitneys.

It seemed to reverberate behind her ribs, and spread out through her bones. "As for what I want, I don't think that's the right question."

"It's the right question if you want me to whirl around in front of you," Becca countered, some recklessness charging through her, making her courageous. "Though I doubt you'll give me the right answer."

"The right question is this—what do you want, and how can I give it to you?" He crossed his arms over his chest, and Becca was distracted by the play of his lean muscles, his corded strength. The man was a deadly weapon, and she felt as if she'd already sustained a body blow.

"I want to fund my sister's Ivy League education," Becca said, wrenching her gaze back to his, ordering herself to concentrate. "I don't much care if you give me money or they do. I only know that I can't do it myself." The unfairness of it almost choked her then, the sheer injustice that allowed worthless human beings like Bradford and Helen so much money, so much easy access to things like a college education—things they probably took for granted—while Becca fought to make her rent each month. It was maddening.

"Then the only other question is, how far are you willing to go to get what you want?" Theo asked softly, his gaze still so intent on hers, still managing to make her feel as if they were all alone in the room—the world.

"Emily deserves the best," Becca said fiercely. "I'll do whatever I have to do to make sure she gets it."

Life wasn't fair. Becca didn't begrudge a single thing she'd had to do. But she wouldn't stand by and watch Emily's dreams slip away when they didn't have to. Not when she'd vowed to her mother that she'd never let that happen. Not when Becca could do something to fix it. Even if it was this.

"I admire ruthlessness and ambition in a woman," Theo said, but there was a grim satisfaction in his voice that Becca didn't understand. Yet she had no difficulty whatsoever understanding him when he raised that hand of his again, and once more motioned for her to spin around.

"It must be nice to be so ridiculously rich that you can barter an entire four years' worth of tuition for one little twirl," Becca said, resisting the urge to fidget, to bite at her lip. She recognized, on some level, that she was stalling. "But who am I to argue?"

"I don't actually care who you are," Theo replied, his voice hardening, and she understood then that he was not a man to be trifled with, not a man to tease. *Not safe at all,* she chided herself. He was, she understood on some primal level, the most dangerous creature she'd ever encountered. The truth of that blazed in his oddly colored eyes, danced through her and left her breathless. "I care what you look like. Do not make me ask you again. Turn around. I want to see you."

And, unbelievably, Becca turned. She felt a hectic heat flood her cheeks, and a terrifying dampness prickle behind her eyes, but she did as she was told. Her heart thudded hard against her chest, humiliation and something else, something that made her tremble even as a sweet ache bloomed to life low in her belly. And still, she slowly pivoted in front of him.

Last time, she had dressed as if she was going to a work interview. A smart, conservative suit. Her best shoes, and her heavy chestnut-colored hair carefully combed back from her face. She'd hated herself, afterward, for trying so hard. This time, she hadn't cared what they might think of her. She didn't even know why they'd summoned her here. So she hadn't bothered to try. She'd worn a ratty pair of jeans, her battered old motorcycle boots, and an old T-shirt beneath an even older hooded sweatshirt. She'd thrown her hair back in a messy ponytail and called it a day. It had been perfectly comfortable on the train, and had had the added benefit of making her snooty relatives cringe when they saw her walk in. She'd been pleased with herself—until now.

Now, she wished she'd worn something else. Something…different. Something that could grab this man's attention, instead of putting that smirk on his frankly sensual mouth. *Why would you want that?* she asked herself, confused by the riot of emotion that surged through her. What was he doing to her? Reeling, she completed the circle, and met his hooded gaze.

"Satisfied?" she asked, with a bravado she wished she felt deep inside of her.

"With the raw materials," he said in that cutting way of his, that somehow made her want to fight him even as, absurdly, it also made her want to please him. "If nothing else."

"I've read that many major CEOs and assorted other captains of industry are sociopaths," she replied, almost conversationally. "I imagine you fit right in."

He really did smile then, and it was so unexpected, so shocking, that Becca actually stepped back. It was as if a fuse blew out inside of her, with a rattle and then a loud pop. His smile lit up that fascinating face of his, making him seem at once more beautiful and more lethal than any man should be.

"Sit down," he said. It was another order. "I have a proposition for you."

"Nothing good has ever followed those words," she

replied, sticking her shaking hands on her hips to hide their state. She did not sit down, despite how fluttery her knees felt beneath her. "It's like checking out the strange noise in a horror movie. It can't possibly end well."

"This is not a horror movie," Theo replied silkily. "This is a simple, if unorthodox, business transaction. Do what I want, and you will receive all you ever wanted and more."

"Let's cut through all this buildup." She smiled at him, fake and hard. "What's the catch? There's always a catch."

For a moment he said nothing, only looked at her, and Becca had the craziest notion that he could see straight into her, that he could read her—that he knew both how determined she was to save her sister's future and how baffled she was by her own reaction to his proximity.

"There are a number of catches," he said, his dark voice soft, his eyes bright. "You will probably dislike many of them, but I suspect you will persevere because you'll be thinking, always, about the end result. About what you will do with all the money we will give you if you do this thing we will ask of you. So none of these catches will matter." His dark brows quirked then. "Save one."

"And what is that?" She had some kind of premonition, perhaps. Or she already knew that this man could—would—devastate her. That he had only refrained from doing so already by sheer coincidence. That it would take so little to undo her. Another smile. Or, God help her, a touch.

She felt the fire between them, and something dark and confining, that seemed to wrap around her like a chain. Like a promise.

His amber-colored eyes seared into her, like molten gold, and she found she could not breathe.

"You will have to obey me," he told her, mercilessly, and not without a certain gleam of male satisfaction in his unholy eyes. "Completely."

CHAPTER TWO

"OBEY YOU?" BECCA repeated, her dismay more than evident on her expressive face. "You mean, like a trained animal?"

"Exactly like a trained animal," he replied. Her eyes were an interesting hazel color, somewhere between green and brown, and they darkened with her emotions. He found himself unduly intrigued. She would have to wear contacts to achieve Larissa's emerald-green shade, he thought, ignoring the shaft of pain that speared through him. "Like a faithful dog at my heel, in fact."

"Clearly you did not rise to your exalted position through sales," she said after a moment, only the faintest catch in her dry voice. "Because your pitch could use some work."

Theo could not decide which was more shocking—the girl's likeness to Larissa, or his own surprising, raging attraction to her. He had never hardened and blazed with need merely *looking* at Larissa. He had wanted her, but not like this. Not with his whole body, in this shower of flame and desire he could not seem to control.

That he should feel these things, while Larissa lay beyond reach, made him loathe himself.

This Becca…did something to him. She infected him,

called out to him, even now when his grief should have made him immune. He could not imagine how he would transform this feral little creature into any believable version of his ethereal, effortlessly chic Larissa. But he was Theo Markou Garcia, crafted from proud Cypriot and Cuban stock. He had done far more impossible things, with far fewer resources. The fact that he stood here at all was proof of that.

And since he did not know how to lose, the only thing he could do was win what was left, as he'd planned.

"What do you know about your cousin Larissa?" he asked quietly. He watched a shadow pass over Becca's face, and her hands balled into fists before she shoved them in the pockets of her jeans.

"What everyone knows," she replied, with a shrug that Theo might have believed was casual had he not seen those telling fists. He felt a sudden surge of sympathy. He knew what those fists meant. He had once balled his own in exactly the same way—pride and anger and determination. He knew exactly what she felt, this stranger with Larissa's face. He wished he did not have to ask her to do something he knew, without a doubt, would bruise the very pride that she clung to with such ferocity. But he had no choice. He had sold his soul long ago, and he could not give up now, not when he was so close. He could not.

"That she is famous for no particular reason," Becca was saying. "That she has too much money and has never had to work for any of it. That there are never any consequences for her bad behavior. And that the tabloids are obsessed with her for some reason, and love nothing more than to follow her from party to party, recording her exploits."

"She is a Whitney," Bradford said in ringing tones

from across the room, the pompous fool. "Whitneys have a certain standing—"

"She's a cautionary tale," Becca retorted, cutting her uncle off. The look she threw at him, and then turned on Theo, was equal parts chilly contempt and a fierce kind of pride that stirred something inside of him. Old memories of another time, another life. His own fists at his sides, his own voice—laced with bravado. "Anytime I am tempted to wish my mother had stayed here and suffered so I might have had an easier life, I simply open the nearest tabloid magazine and remind myself that it is far better to be poor than to be a useless parasite like Larissa Whitney."

Theo winced. He heard Helen suck in a strangled, outraged breath, and a quick glance told him that Bradford's face had turned an alarming shade of red. And yet Becca only gazed up at him, unafraid. Almost triumphant. Theo imagined she'd dreamed of delivering that speech for a long, long time. And why not? She had no doubt been treated shabbily by the mighty Whitneys, like so many others before her, Larissa included. Larissa especially.

Not that it could matter. Not now. Not to Theo. Not to Larissa, who had been lost long before he'd met her, long before she'd fallen so far.

"Larissa collapsed outside a nightclub last Friday night," Theo said coolly, deliberately, watching the way the color changed in Becca's face, the flush of courage dimming. "She is currently in a coma. There is no hope that she will ever recover."

Becca's mouth firmed to a taut line, and Theo could see the way she swallowed, as if her throat was suddenly dry, but she did not look away. He found he could not help but admire that, too.

"I'm sorry," she said quietly. "I did not mean to be cruel." She shook her head slightly, looking uncertain for the first time since she'd met his gaze when he'd walked into the parlor. "I don't understand why I'm here."

"You happen to look enough like Larissa that you could, with some help, pass for her," Theo said, matter-of-factly. "That's why you're here."

Because there was no point wallowing in his grief—no need to dwell on the past. There was only the future and what must happen now. He had given Whitney Media everything he had, everything he was. It was time that he became an owner, not simply an employee. Gaining Larissa's controlling interest would, with one stroke, make him the living embodiment of the American Dream. Rags to riches, just as he'd promised his mother before her death. Perhaps not exactly as he'd planned, but close enough. Even without Larissa.

"Pass for her?" Becca repeated, as if she could not make sense of the words.

"Larissa has a certain number of shares in Whitney Media," Bradford said from his position on the couch, his voice completely devoid of emotion, as if he was not talking about his only child. Theo felt himself stiffen, and forced himself to let it go. None of that could matter now. "When she and Theo got engaged—"

At this, Becca's eyes flew to his. Theo merely lifted a brow.

"I thought she was dating that actor," Becca said stiffly. "The one who dates all the models and heiresses."

"You should not believe everything you read," Theo said with a careless shrug, and then wondered why he'd bothered. It was still so new, perhaps. He was still defending Larissa's honor, when he knew perfectly well that if it was not that actor, it would have been another one. Or both. He still didn't know what that made him. A fool, certainly. But he'd made that decision a long time ago, hadn't he? If he wanted what she represented—and he had, he did—then he had to allow her to be who she was. He had to let her do as she pleased. And so he had. The end was more important than the means, he'd always thought.

"Larissa made Theo a gift of a significant amount of her shares," Bradford was saying. "It would give him a controlling interest in the company. It was meant to be a wedding present."

"I believe they call that a dowry," Becca said, her disgust plain in her flashing eyes, the lift of her chin. "How quaint, in this day and age."

"It was a gift," Theo replied, his voice more clipped than it should have been. As if this stranger's opinion mattered. "Not a dowry." He had never apologized for going after what he wanted, using any means necessary. He would not start now.

"The terms were laid out explicitly in the prenuptial agreement," Bradford continued. "The shares were to go to Theo upon their wedding day, or in the unfortunate event of her death. But we have reason to believe she altered her will."

"Why would she alter her will?" Becca asked. She looked from Bradford to Theo and then back again, judgment plain on her face. *Because of you, obviously,* her expression read.

"My daughter has long been preyed upon by the unsavory," Bradford said, in the first faux-fatherly tone Theo had heard from him since they'd received the call on Friday night. From anyone else, it might have been believable. "There's a certain ne'er-do-well who would do anything to get his hands on Larissa's shares. We think he succeeded."

"That's where you come in," Theo said then, close enough to see the angry flash in Becca's eyes when she looked at him. Close enough to feel his own shocking, searing reaction to it. *Sex,* he thought. This was about sex. He simply hadn't expected it from this woman, under these circumstances. It was the surprise that was throwing him, he told himself. That was all. The odd similarities between her and the man he'd been once upon a time were simply coincidence, nothing more.

"I can't imagine how," she said, her voice cold. "What could I possibly have to do with a situation that already seems too complicated?"

"We cannot find a copy of the new version of her will." Theo watched the muted emotions move over her face, and wished he could read them. Wished he could simply bend her to his will as he did most people. But that would come. "We think her lover has the only existing copy."

"And you can't ask him to show it to you, though the poor girl lies in a *coma?*" Becca sounded incredulous. And condemning, in equal measure. "Is this a soap opera?"

"I want you to pretend to be Larissa," Theo said, because nothing could be gained by beating around the bush. There was too much at stake. All the long years of single-minded focus, determination. The bitter acceptance that once his usefulness as Larissa's *wrong side of the tracks* lover had ended, their relationship had become purely business, cold and complicated. His searing, implacable focus on the end goal no matter what. "I want you to be so good at it that you fool her lover. And I want you to get me that will."

There was a long, heavy silence, broken only by Helen's delicate sniffles into her monogrammed handkerchief. Becca stared at him for a long, almost uncomfortable moment, as if her not-quite-green eyes could see into the parts of him he'd thought he'd buried long ago, and then she let out a sound that was a shade too hollow to be a laugh.

"No," she said, simple and to the point.

Her refusal lay there for a moment, seeming to fill the elegant room, blocking out the late-afternoon light that poured in through the soaring windows.

"That's it?" Theo asked softly, not sure he could believe what he'd heard. Not sure when someone had last said no to him, for that matter. Even Larissa had always said *yes,* no matter what she'd then gone on to do. "That's all you have to say?"

"That is not, by any stretch of the imagination, all I have to say," Becca threw back at him, her temper flaring in her that suddenly. It lit up her face, made it suddenly unlike Larissa's—and yet remarkably, shockingly attractive. "But it is all I plan to say. You're crazy." She looked back at her aunt and uncle, her lips curling. "You're all crazy. I've never been happier in my life that you people don't claim me."

And then she turned, her spine as straight as a queen's, her head high, and walked through the door without looking back, more elegant in her ratty clothes than some debutantes looked in their opulent ball gowns. Looking just like Larissa at her haughtiest.

Bradford and Helen broke into a loud, angry noise, but Theo barely heard them.

She was magnificent, and, more to the point, she could be Larissa.

He was not about to let her get away.

* * *

Becca knew he would be the one to follow her, so she did not have to turn to identify the speaker when she heard the quiet command from behind her.

"Stop," he said again.

Once more, she found herself obeying him without meaning to do so. She scowled at the marble floor beneath her feet, as if it was the fault of the stone she had an apparent weakness for this man.

"I do not have to follow your orders simply because you issue them," she said, as if she had not already done so. "There is no agreement between us."

"Your tender sensibilities do you credit, I'm sure," Theo said. His voice was too dark, and wove far too many complicated patterns down the back of her neck, through her stomach, and even down to the soles of her feet. She knew that keeping her back to him was a mistake, that she begged for her own destruction that way.

But when she turned, he was right there in front of her, so dark and impossibly bright-eyed in the vast entry hall, so hopelessly compelling, and she was not sure that there was any way at all to be safe around this man. No matter what her treacherous mind whispered, as if it could discern something in him that was otherwise hidden—as if it wanted her to lay down her defenses then and there, on faith. But she had none. Not while she stood in the Whitney mansion, surrounded by enemies.

"I doubt that you really mean to compliment me," she said, searching the angles and planes of his fascinating, addictive face for clues. "I suspect you only do so when you are preparing to throw your weight around."

"The difference between me and whoever it is you think I am," Theo said in that low, disturbingly sensual voice, his mouth crooking slightly, "is that I don't have to throw my weight around to achieve my ends. My will is usually sufficient."

"I'm so sorry to ruin your winning streak," she murmured with cloying insincerity. "But I prefer my will to yours."

He shrugged slightly, as if he could not bother to worry about the force of her will, so puny was it next to his own. "I'm depending on your practicality," he said quietly. "I suspect it will win out before you make the great mistake of walking out that door."

She didn't know why she stood there so tensely, braced for attack, when he stood a few feet away and looked very nearly idle. In the way that great predators allowed themselves to appear idle moments before they pounced.

"Is this more of your sales pitch?" she asked. "I'm not interested. You and those people are nothing more than ghouls, waiting for that poor girl to die—"

"You know nothing about her," he interrupted her, the rebuke in his voice not at all lessened by the smoothness of the delivery. "Nor about anything else that goes on in this family, or this company."

"I don't want to know anything about any of you!" she retorted, wondering why it should sting to hear him state the simple truth so baldly. Because, of course, he was right. She knew nothing about the family that had categorically rejected her since before her birth. "I don't want to have another thought about any one of you the moment I walk out that door!"

He moved closer, his eyes glowing like embers, and she knew then, as her stomach tied itself into an aching knot, that he was truly a devil, this man. And that if she was not careful, he could have a power over her she'd never given anyone. But even so, she did not step back. She did not try to protect herself as she knew she should.

"The only person I want you to think about is your sister," he said, in that voice of his, so dark, so sinful, that it seemed to move inside of her without her will.

"I always think about my sister, thank you," she managed to say.

"Can you really pass up the opportunity to secure her future?" he asked, so reasonably. So calmly. "All because it suits you to feel morally superior to the family who denied you for so long?"

It was a hit straight to the heart, and he knew it. She could see that he knew it as she stared at him, stricken, and his remarkable eyes gleamed.

"Does it help your sister that you leave here with your righteous indignation firmly in place?" he asked in that same deadly calm way of his. "Or do you suppose, years down the line, that she might be somewhat more grateful for the Ivy League education you will deny her if you walk out now?"

The cold marble hall seemed to seep into her, chilling her. Her throat felt dusty, and there was that dangerous heat in her eyes. And he was right, damn him. She wanted to feel better about herself, to be better than *them,* but she wanted Emily's future—Emily's happiness—more. She'd promised her mother. She'd *promised.*

And wasn't that why she'd come here in the first place? Wasn't that why she'd put all of this into motion? How could she back out now, just because she didn't like the terms? She'd known from the start that she wouldn't like anything about these people. Why was she running away just because they were confirming her worst opinion of them now?

"You've made your point," she said finally, when she could not bear the way he looked at her a moment longer—as if he knew exactly what she thought, what she felt. As if he'd manipulated this entire situation to reach this point, because it suited him. He was the most terrifying man she'd ever met—because he was so powerful, but even more because part of her thrilled to it, and wanted to melt right there in front of him. Wanted to surrender to the whispers in her own head, and pretend he might keep her safe rather than crush her.

But she would never let that happen. Accepting a situation and using it to further her own ends was not the same thing as surrendering. She wouldn't let it be.

"I want Emily's entire education assured," she said, her voice clipped and tense to her own ears. "Freshman year through a postdoctoral degree, should she want one."

"You'll get your mother's entire inheritance," Theo said at once, almost offhandedly. As if he spoke of a minor allowance rather than a stunning fortune. His amber gaze seemed to bore into her, into her darkest, most secret places, taking her breath. "Everything that was taken from her, plus interest, from the day she left to give birth to you."

Becca refused to let him see how that got to her, how the guilt still ate at her no matter how she told herself she should not feel it, that Caroline had made her own choices, and so she fought to keep her face, her voice, impassive.

"In writing, of course," she clarified. "You'll understand if I don't trust you. Anything connected to the Whitney family is tainted."

"My lawyers are standing by," he replied in that deceptively easy way of his, as if this were not her soul they were discussing. "All you need to do is sign."

She had the sense that she had gotten lost, somehow, without seeming to stray from the path. That she was in a dark woods, and there was no hope of sunlight. He watched her, his dark face and glowing eyes like some kind of beacon, beckoning to her, and she had the sudden panicked thought that if she did this, if she crossed this line, if she spent even one more second in this man's company, she might as well write herself off entirely.

Because he would change her. Not just because he wanted her to pretend to be his comatose fiancée, which was morally questionable enough. But because he was... too much. Too dark. Too powerful. Too outside anything she'd ever experienced. How could she possibly handle this man? She couldn't even handle this conversation!

But she thought again of Emily, and knew she had no choice. She had the means to set her sister free. She would do it. She had held her mother's hand in that hospital bed, looked into her eyes, and she had promised.

"All right," she said, and though her voice didn't quite echo, it seemed to reverberate somehow, as if the world was changing all around her as she spoke. Or perhaps that was just the way his eyes gleamed, with heat and triumph, as he looked at her. As he won. "What do you want me to do?"

CHAPTER THREE

"I TRUST YOU were discreet," Theo said in his intent, focused way, lounging with an indolence she could not quite believe in the back of the car that had met Becca's flight. "As you agreed to be in the papers you signed."

He had given her twenty-four hours to get her affairs in order.

Twenty-four hours to make sure Emily could stay with her best friend's family while Becca "went away on business," which Emily had done many times before while Becca worked on a trial—and this was certainly a kind of trial, wasn't it? Twenty-four hours to explain to her employers that she needed the time off she'd saved up over the years—and that she needed it immediately, for "family reasons," and no, she didn't know when she'd be back.

She didn't like to lie, but what could she tell her younger sister? Or the boss who had helped her out time and again while she'd struggled to raise Emily in the years after her mother's death? How could she explain what she was doing when she hardly understood it herself? Twenty-four hours to pack a single, small bag and wonder why she bothered—especially when Theo had smirked and told her not to worry about a wardrobe, that it would be provided. His unsaid *because yours is embarrassing to people like us* seemed to singe her ears, making her flush with anger every time she thought of it. Of him.

Which she did with depressing, alarming regularity.

Twenty-four hours and then she was back in New York. This time, to stay. To become her cousin, a woman she had always comfortably disdained from afar.

Twenty-four hours, Becca discovered, was not very much time at all to prepare for your whole world to change.

"No," she said now, pretending to be calm. Pretending that she had been inside a flashy limousine a million times before, and was thus unmoved by the casual opulence evident in the plush seats, the glossy wood-paneling, the crystal decanters. "I took out several ads in the *Boston Globe* and appeared on CNN to discuss our little deal."

"Very amusing," Theo said, in a tone that suggested he found her anything but. And yet that gleam in his amber gaze made her think he understood her, somehow. *Wishful thinking,* she told herself sharply. "I'm sure that kind of sarcasm serves you well in your chosen career." Could he sound any more dismissive? Any more snide? As if *paralegal* was a synonym for *prostitute?*

Although perhaps she was in no position to cast stones, since she was sitting here for money, wasn't she?

"I'm usually praised more for my work ethic than my wit," Becca replied, clenching her hands together in her lap and forcing a tight smile. "Did you become the CEO of Whitney Media by telling silly jokes? I thought that kind of power had more to do with destroying lives and worshipping the almighty dollar above all things, including your own soul."

"Oh," he said softly, "I sold my soul. Have no doubt about that. But it was too long ago to matter now."

"I think you'll find that soullessness suits only those in your position," Becca replied as if the flash in his gaze affected her not at all, as if she did not fight off a shiver. "The rest of us are preoccupied with, among other things, *being human*."

They had wanted to send the private jet; Becca had insisted on flying coach on a commercial flight. It was, she'd thought, the last chance she'd have to do something *normal* for some time. And it was probably her last little rebellion, too.

But the flight had allowed her the time to think about what she was about to do, and something had solidified inside of her as the plane winged south along the eastern seaboard. She would step into this world, she told herself, the world of the Whitneys, to secure her sister's future and to keep her promise to her mother. But it would be more than that. She would prove, once and for all, that they were all better off for being discarded and ignored. She would never again torture herself with questions about what her life might have been like had her mother stayed in New York, or whether Caroline's great sacrifice had been in vain. She would never have to *wonder* again.

It would be worth almost any indignity to walk back out of the Whitney's glittering, poisonous world with that knowledge secure inside of her. She could almost feel the satisfaction of it, in advance. She'd felt a sense of anticipation as she'd exited the plane, closer and closer to her fate with every step.

And still something in her had thrilled to the sight of a black-clad driver holding a sign with her name on it in the Baggage Claim. Some part of her had been more impressed than it should have been when the driver had taken her bag and escorted her to the waiting vehicle, gleaming black and expensive at the curb, in clear and arrogant violation of the strict No Parking regulations.

She had not expected Theo to be inside, sprawled out across the backseat, dressed in a dark-colored suit, which only called attention to the lean power of his big body. He was still far too dangerous, far too disturbing. She'd forgotten to breathe. And then his arresting, amber-colored eyes had fixed on her, sending electricity charging through her, lighting her up from the inside out.

She'd rather die than show him her reaction to his nearness—her reaction to being alone with him in an enclosed space. She thought she might die anyway, from the wild pounding of her heart, the shiver in her limbs and the trembling in her core. She wanted to believe her reaction came from trepidation, from fear of the world she was now going to have to learn how to live in, at least for a little while. The world that had chewed her mother up and spit her out. She might know deep inside that she would conquer it, but she still first had to survive it. She told herself it was nothing more than that.

He watched her for a moment, something not quite a smile flirting with his hard mouth, something too close to soft in his gaze. "I cannot imagine how you've come by your dire opinion of me," he said after a long moment. "We've only just met."

"You make quite an impression," Becca said honestly, wishing that were not true. Wishing she was not so *aware* of him, that every cell in her body did not seem to sing out that awareness.

"You are supposed to be impressed," he said, with

a sardonic inflection she had to fight to ignore. "If not wholly overawed."

"Oh, I am," Becca replied at once, forcing herself to remember who she was. Why she was here. What she had to do. She squared her shoulders. "Though in contrast to your usual minions, I imagine, I'm a bit more awed by your conceit and arrogance than I am by your supposed magnificence."

The curve of his mouth became a smile. "So noted," he said.

His gaze warmed, and she warmed, too, and then wondered from one beat of her heart to the next what it would be like if he weren't one of them. If he weren't the enemy. If that look she'd glimpsed in his gaze now and again truly meant something. But that was ridiculous.

He shifted slightly in his seat. He was much too close.

"It's too bad you've chosen to hate everyone you meet on this adventure so indiscriminately, Rebecca."

"It's Becca," she said, ignoring the slight catch in her throat, the wild fluttering of her pulse. "And I would hardly call my feelings on the Whitney family and anyone tainted by a close association with them *indiscriminate*. It's a reasonable response to who they are, I think. It's also common sense."

There was a slight, tense pause. The air seemed to contract around them.

"Everyone is more complicated than they appear on the surface," Theo said finally in a soft voice. "You'd do well to remember that."

"I'm not complicated at all," Becca retorted, leaning back in the seat and crossing her legs, taking a perverse sort of pride in the look of distaste Theo fixed on her old jeans and battered boots. "What you see is exactly what you get."

"Good lord," Theo said, sweeping that same look over her whole body, from her feet to her hair. "I certainly hope not."

Becca bristled, but tried to hide it behind a smile. "Is that how you go about winning people over?" she demanded. "Because I have to tell you, your approach needs work."

"I don't have to win you over," he said, his own smile sharpening, those impossible eyes boring into her, making her fight against the urge to squirm in her seat. "I've already bought you."

Theo lived in a vast two-story penthouse in Tribeca. He led Becca out of the most luxuriously appointed elevator she'd ever seen and into a wide, private marble lobby that opened into another entryway, accented with white-painted brick walls and graceful shelves holding art, books and various artifacts that struck Becca as decidedly Mediterranean. The entryway opened up into a great room with a ceiling two stories above, stretching out before her toward high, arching windows that led out to a wide brick terrace and beyond that, Manhattan itself in all its high-thrusting, slick glory.

She had never felt farther away from her tiny apartment in its not-so-great part of Boston.

The Whitney mansion had been easier to accept, somehow. Her mother had told stories of what it had been like to grow up in that house, and summer in another equally extravagant home in Newport, Rhode Island, so perhaps Becca had expected mythical modern castles on Fifth Avenue. It was just one more part of the Whitney mystique. But all that was inherited opulence, handed down from one Whitney to the next ever since the glory days of their Gilded Age friends and contemporaries, American royalty like the Carnegies, Rockefellers, and Vanderbilts.

But this…this was something else. Real people, Becca thought almost numbly, still looking around in awe, didn't actually live like *this*.

Except Theo seemed perfectly at home. He had his cell phone to his ear and was murmuring something in an undertone as he sauntered through the elegant room, seemingly unmoved by the sheer luxury all around him. And yet Becca knew without a single doubt that it was all of his design—from the richly colored Oriental rugs at her feet, stretching across hardwood floors polished to a gleam, to the furniture she did not have to be told was incredibly expensive, all of it seeming to belong exactly where it was, as if it had grown there, mahoganies and blacks and scarlets, and all of it inviting, not stuffy. Her gaze rested for a moment on the set of deep, lush-looking sofas in one corner, set to take advantage of the fireplace and the dizzying view. There was interesting art on the walls and the shelves were lined with important-looking books and more intriguing objects—vases, small boxes, statues. A wrought iron spiral stair wound up to the floor above, that boasted an open gallery to take advantage of the great room's vastness. Opulence and invitation, everywhere she turned.

Was she really expected to stay here? With a man who walked through this room as if it were common-place, unworthy of his notice? A cold shiver worked its way down her spine, making goose bumps rise up in response. Who would she be when all of this was over? Because she knew, once again, on some deep, incontrovertible level, that what she'd put into motion by agreeing to be here would change her forever. *What would be left?* a small voice asked inside of her. *Who would she be when she'd finished playing Larissa?*

You will be yourself, she reminded herself sternly. *Finally free of the notion that these people are important to you in any way—that they matter at all.*

"Muriel will show you to your rooms," he said, startling her when he stopped and turned. She was suddenly afraid that her mouth really had dropped open and that she'd been gaping at the things he owned like a country bumpkin. Like the poor relation to his wealthy employers that she, in fact, was.

As for the other things she'd been thinking, well— she shrugged them off. It was too late now, anyway. She was here. The papers were signed. And Emily needed this. More than that, *she* needed to do this for Emily, so Emily would never have to do anything like this, with these horrible people, herself.

She needed to make her mother proud, in whatever way she could, even all these years later. She owed her mother's memory at least that much. *At least.*

And she would walk out of here with her head high, knowing exactly who she was. With all of the Whitney legacy firmly behind her. Finally.

Swallowing hard, she turned to the woman she hadn't even seen enter the room from somewhere off to the left. The kitchen? Servants' quarters? Narnia? Nothing would surprise her, at this point.

"I need to take a few calls, but I will come find you in about forty-five minutes," Theo said, his voice all business, matter-of-fact. It made her realize that he had not been using that voice before, in the car. Or at the Whitney mansion. She frowned.

"Fine," she said, her thoughts too muddled to say

anything else. Why would this situation be anything but business to him? Why should his voice alter at all? Had she not imagined that softer look after all?

His amber eyes flicked over her, making clench her fists in unconscious response as her heart thumped painfully hard in her chest, an answer to her silently asked questions that she refused to acknowledge.

"Our first order of business will be your hair," he said, those captivating, intriguing eyes narrowing slightly as he looked at her.

She reached up to touch the end of her chestnut-colored ponytail automatically, but she wasn't surprised. Larissa was as famous for her peroxide-blond mane as she was for her questionable behavior and pointless existence. Becca hadn't really thought through the specific details of this charade, but dying her hair made sense.

"Will you be making me a blonde yourself?" she asked, meaning to sound dry and arch, but her voice came out much softer, much more uncertain, than she'd intended, as she found herself imagining those strong hands in her hair, against her scalp.

His gaze seemed to darken, and it was worse than the usual kick of amber—it seemed to creep inside of her and turn her into something knotted and raw. She had to remind herself to breathe.

"I will make you exactly what you have to be," he said. As if he'd heard her worst fears. As if she'd spoken them aloud. His dark head tilted slightly to one side. "The question is whether or not you can handle it."

"I can handle anything," she threw at him, feeling goaded beyond her endurance—and yet he only stood there, so calmly powerful, and watched her. It made panic—and something much hotter, much darker—roar through her, blistering everything in its path.

"We'll see, won't we?"

And with that, Theo Markou Garcia was gone, leaving Becca feeling overwhelmed—and something else, something she refused to call *bereft*—in the middle of the vast, beautiful room.

"Come," Muriel said, and led Becca off to her doom.

Blonde, she was even more of a threat, Theo thought with a mixture of temper and resignation.

And then wondered why he'd used that word, as feelings he did not care to identify coursed through him. *Threat.* How could she possibly be a *threat?* He was Theo Markou Garcia and she…she was whatever he made her. He stared at the girl as she sat before the mirror in the guest suite he'd allocated her. She was looking at herself with her cloudy-green eyes dark. She looked fragile and a little unnerved, as if she did not know what she'd gotten herself into.

But most of all, she looked like Larissa.

Françoise was a hairdressing genius—known for her discretion even without the giant sum Theo had paid her to ensure her silence—and had created a true masterpiece. The hair was a symphony of blondes, from a sun-kissed pale shade to the lightest honey, cascading around her like an effortless blonde wave and framing the face that was undeniably Larissa's.

Larissa, but with fire and emotion in her eyes. Larissa, but so much more *alive.* So much more aware. Not anesthetized and dull-eyed.

She was like a ghost in reverse, this girl, with her raggedy clothes and her off-color eyes, eyes that should have been green and were instead that mossy, changeable hazel, like a version of Larissa that had never been. Her nose, perhaps, was more narrow. Her chin was a touch stronger, her lips fuller. But he had to search out the differences. He had to look hard to see them. If he didn't know better, he would have assumed this was Larissa Whitney herself.

No one would look at this woman and think she was anything but the real thing. Because no one saw what they did not expect to see. Theo knew this better than anyone. He had fought against the markers of his humble beginnings most of his life, until he'd met Larissa and had used that very roughness to hide behind. She'd thought she was taking home the kind of man her parents would hate, yet one more of her rebellions. She'd had no idea how ambitious Theo was. Not at first.

"It is an extraordinary likeness," he said, because he had stared too long, and he could see the nerves Becca struggled to hide. He even sympathized. He remembered how nervous he'd been when Larissa had first noticed him, when she'd chosen him—and how cold he'd gone inside when he finally understood that she wanted only to use him to infuriate and appall Bradford. Just as he remembered what it had taken to turn instead into Bradford's favorite. She'd never forgiven him.

He could see himself in the mirror, hovering behind her like some great Gothic brute—but he shook himself. That was the way Larissa had made him feel. Like the hulking, ill-mannered swine before whom her pearls were unfairly cast. Yet this was not Larissa. This was only a facsimile of her, and *this* woman had no greater claim to gentility than he did. Less, perhaps, since this was Manhattan and money made its own friends, especially when it was coupled with so much power and the blue-blooded Whitney stamp of authenticity, heritage and rank.

But oh, how he wished this woman were the real thing. And that she was his.

"I never really noticed it before," Becca said quietly, turning her head from side to side. He might have thought she was calm, had he not been able to see the way her knee bounced in agitation. A nervous tic he would have to work on, he thought. Larissa had never been nervous. She had redefined *languid*.

He hated that she lay so helpless, and he was reduced to the *past tense*. It seemed suddenly terribly unfair that this woman—this pretender—should be so vibrant, sparkle with so much energy, when Larissa could not and would not, ever again. That Becca could be free of all that had weighted Larissa down, ruined her. That she should be so much like Larissa had been so long ago, when he'd first seen her—or in any case, as he'd thought Larissa had been back then, before he'd known her.

"I find that difficult to believe," he said, dismissively. He reminded himself to be patient, to tamp down the mess of his emotions as was his way; that this was a process, not a race. "Larissa is a world-renowned beauty. Therefore, with your bone structure and likeness to her, you are, too."

Her gaze met his in the mirror's reflection. Held. "As it happens, I am a whole, entire person in my own right." Her brows rose, challenging him, as far from Larissa's deflecting smiles and easy laughter as it was possible to get. And despite himself, he wanted her. He felt her in his sex, his blood. "I have a life that has never, and will never, have anything to do with my resemblance to Larissa Whitney. In fact," she said, turning around on the vanity bench to face him, her eyes wild with temper, "I'll let you in on a little secret. In *most* places, Larissa Whitney is the punch line to a joke."

"I suggest you do not tell that joke here," Theo said, mildly enough, but he saw the color bloom in her cheeks. It seemed to echo in him, seemed to pound through him like need, like *want*—because Larissa had never responded to him. She had tolerated him, waved him away, pretended to be polite if there were witnesses nearby—but she'd never *reacted* to him. Not as a woman should respond to a man. Not like this.

But he could not let himself think of that truth.

He should not want this ghost. It was the worst betrayal, surely. Hadn't he vowed to Larissa that he would never treat her that way, no matter what she did? No matter how she treated him in return? What kind of man was he to ignore that now? He should only want Becca for what her face could bring him, what he deserved after all these years of Larissa's games and broken promises. But his body was not paying attention to him. At all.

"There's no going back now, is there?" Becca asked. Or perhaps it was not really a question. "You've made me into her. Congratulations."

Theo smiled slightly. "I've had your hair done like hers," he corrected her. "Let's not get ahead of ourselves. There is the matter of your wardrobe—and, of course, your entire personal history."

"It hurts me to say this," she said, temper crackling in her voice, "but I am, genetically, just as much of a Whitney as she is. I simply wasn't waited on hand and foot my entire life."

"But she was," he said brusquely, as much to curtail the decidedly carnal turn of his thoughts as to reprimand her. "And therein lies one of the major differences we must smooth over if you are to pass as her. Larissa went to Spence and Choate, and then Brown. She spent her summers sailing in Newport, when she wasn't traveling the world. You did none of these things." He shrugged. "This is not a value judgment, you understand—this is a statement of fact."

"It's true," Becca said. Her knee began jumping again, and as if she could not bear to let him see it, she moved to her feet, tossing her gleaming blonde hair back from her face in a move that was so much like Larissa's that it made Theo suck in a sharp breath, past and present colliding too suddenly, and not pleasantly. But the arch of her brows, the tilt of her head—so challenging, so fierce—that was all Becca.

"My mother died three days after my eighteenth birthday," she said with no trace at all of emotion, just that blaze of green in her eyes and that scathing heat beneath her words. "My sister and I think of that as lucky—because if I hadn't been eighteen, they would have taken her from me. I had to scrape and save and figure out a way to take care of myself and Emily, because no one else was going to. Certainly not Larissa or her family, who could have saved us a thousand times over, but chose not to, even though they were notified. Maybe they were too busy *sailing* in Newport."

Her words hung in the air, condemnation and curse, and Theo wanted things he couldn't have. Just as he always had, though he had gone to such lengths to make sure that nothing—and no one—would ever be out of his reach again. He told himself it was simply his knee-jerk reaction to a woman who looked like this, telling him what hurt her. He wanted to take away her pain. He wanted to rescue her. From the Whitneys. From the past. And it didn't matter, because she was not Larissa, and Larissa had never allowed that, anyway. She would have scoffed at the thought.

"They probably didn't care," Theo said coldly, brutally, as much to snap himself back to reality as to slap her down.

He watched her pale, and sway very slightly on her feet—and for a moment he hated himself, because if anyone could understand the contours and complexity of her bitterness, it was him. And he did. But there were bigger things at play here. He *could not* lose sight of his goals. He never had, not since his desperate boyhood in the worst Miami neighborhoods. Not even when it might have saved his relationship with Larissa. Once he got those shares, he would be an *owner*. He would be one of *them*. He would be more than the hired help. Finally. He would do anything—had done anything—to make that a reality.

"Just as I do not care," he continued in the same way, though he did not care for how it made him feel. "This is not a forum for your grievances against the Whitney family. This is not a therapy session."

"You are a pig." She spat out the words and in that sentiment, he thought with some trace of black humor, she was exactly like Larissa.

"I don't care what you think of your cousin's privileges, or her pampered existence, or her family," he said, forcing himself to continue in that same heavy-handed way, making sure there was no doubt about how things stood. *Start as you mean to go on,* he told himself—and he could not let this woman get to him, manipulate him. Make him care. Just like Larissa had done, and look how that had ended up. "I'm sure their wealth and carelessness offends you. It doesn't matter. The only thing that matters is turning you into her, and I can't do that if you waste our time telling me how much more meaningful your life is than hers, and how much harder you've struggled. *I don't care.* Do you understand?"

"Perfectly." Her voice was clipped. Her face was pale, though a hectic color shone in her dark hazel eyes. *Hatred,* he thought. It was nothing new.

What was new was that he wanted so much to change it.

"Wonderful," he said. He let himself smile slightly, as if she did not get to him already, no matter what rules he'd tried to institute. As if he did not have the highly unusual urge to apologize to her, to make it better—or to make her understand. As if he really was the dark, forbidding monster he had no doubt at all she believed him to be. Hadn't he gone to great lengths to make it so? "Let's get started."

CHAPTER FOUR

"YOU MUST LOVE HER very much," Becca said at breakfast a week later, without knowing she meant to speak. But it was done, and her words hung there, seeming to fill up the space between them out on the terrace, rebounding back from the skyscrapers that towered all around them. But her words had as little effect on Theo Markou Garcia as the blazing heat lamps that kept off the March chill, as this man acknowledged no weather that did not suit him. She stabbed her grapefruit with the strange, serrated-edged spoon that had been provided for that singular purpose and continued grimly on. "If you are willing to go to such lengths to recreate her. Like Frankenstein's bride."

"Am I patching you together from bits and pieces? A carcass here, a limb or two there?" Theo asked without looking up from the sleek laptop computer he carried everywhere with him, and which Becca suspected was his real, true love. "I think my final product, at the very least, will be a bit smoother and more attractive in appearance than Frankenstein's."

There it was again—that hint that somewhere beneath his dark, impenetrable male beauty lurked a man with a sense of humor. Becca sometimes thought she was more likely to wake up one morning and believe herself

to be Larissa Whitney in the flesh than Theo was to
actually…be funny. Crack a real smile. Relax. Despite
the evidence now and again to the contrary.

But then again, she told herself, not for the first time,
the man was undoubtedly grieving in some distinctly
wealthy male way that was lost on her. He obviously
had strong feelings about Larissa. At the very least, he'd
studied her so completely that, as he'd demonstrated over
the past seven days, he could dissect the ways Becca was
not her in excruciating detail.

"Slouch more," he said now, barely sparing her a
glance as he kept tapping away at his keyboard, no
doubt buying and selling whole countries at a keystroke.
"Larissa did not sit so straight in her chair, like an overly
enthusiastic high school student. She was jaded. Bored.
She reclined, and waited to be served."

Becca curved her spine back into the wrought iron
chair, and lounged like a dissolute pasha. Like *him*.

"She sounds delightful," she said dryly. "As ever."

It had been a long week.

Becca was not an actor and had never tried to be
one, so perhaps this was simply a part of the actor's job
that she had never considered before—but she had been
taken aback to discover that Theo wanted her to research
every aspect of Larissa's life as if she could expect to
be quizzed upon it at any moment, from any quarter.

"I don't remember who *I* was friends with in the
sixth grade," she'd protested, while sitting before the
stacks of notes and photographs, papers and yearbooks
that Theo had compiled for her review—all of it spread
across the polished mahogany table in the book-studded
library, almost covering it completely. She'd looked over
at Theo, who sat with that merciless expression on his
hard face in one of the deep leather chairs near the

stone fireplace, playing idly with the globe in a brass stand next to him, his big frame deceptively relaxed-looking.

"I suspect that you would," he'd replied, entirely unperturbed, "if those friends included Rockefellers, movie stars and minor European royalty."

And what argument was there to that? Becca had gritted her teeth, and started to read what he'd put in front of her—uncovering the facts of Larissa Whitney's life, page by page. She'd tried not to notice that said facts seemed like little more than a dream of the high life to someone like Becca. European tours, stints in Hawaii and exclusive ranches near the Rocky Mountains. The Maldives for Easter, the Hamptons for weekend parties. New Year's parties in old Cape Cod mansions and more low-key vacations at the family beachside estate in Newport. Horseback riding, ballroom dancing classes, French and Italian lessons at the hands of private tutors; name the luxury, and Larissa had been handed it on the proverbial silver platter. Over and over again.

The more Becca read about the way Larissa, only a year or so older than she was, had been raised, the harder it was to soldier on. But she did.

The days had fallen into a certain routine. Up early for breakfast with Theo, and his latest round of casual personal insults couched as constructive advice on bettering her Larissa impression. Then an hour in the private, state-of-the-art gym—located near Theo's office on the first floor of the penthouse—with the most sadistic personal trainer imaginable: Theo himself.

"I am already in perfectly fine shape," she'd gritted out at him, when he'd decreed she should lift a heavier set of weights before running another set of intervals on his treadmill. Becca had come to loathe that treadmill.

"No one is debating that," he'd said. The way his gaze had flicked over her then seemed to leave scorch marks, making her wish she'd had on a head-to-toe cloak instead of a skimpy tank top over running shorts—even as the body he seemed to view so dispassionately had reacted to him against her will. Her core had softened, her skin had begun tingling. "But we are not talking about the reality before us here, we are talking about the accepted aesthetic in the circles Larissa ran in."

"You mean the kinds of circles that don't eat food of any kind and have wildly expensive recreational drug hobbies?" she'd thrown back at him.

"Larissa used to model in her spare time, Rebecca," he'd said in that cutting way, as if mocking her for thinking she had the right to her own opinion. "I don't know if you've looked at the fashion magazines lately, but *emaciated* is, unfortunately, the preferred look. You are not nearly skeletal enough."

"My name," she had said, panting from a toxic combination of rage, running and his dazzling proximity in his gym shorts and a soft T-shirt that made love to his hard pectorals, "is *Becca*."

"Run faster," he'd advised her softly. "Talk less."

He was a maddening, impossible man. That was the conclusion she'd reached in the long days of her first week in his relentless presence. The endless hours of Larissa Studies, followed by afternoons of clothes, makeup, and what Theo called *finishing school* with his usual sardonic inflection. That involved trying on pieces of Larissa's wardrobe—all of it too small, too revealing, or too outlandish for Becca—and learning how to dress and act like Larissa had under his ever-critical eye.

"This dress looks ridiculous," she'd muttered, plucking at the odd concoction that seemed to be all ruffle, no dress. "Where would anyone go in something like this?"

"That is a custom-made Valentino gown," Theo had replied smoothly, his dark brows rising, as if shocked to the core that Becca hadn't known that at a glance.

"I don't care what it is," Becca had replied, flushing with embarrassment at once again being proved so small, so provincial, and yet determined never to admit that. Never. She glared at him through the full-length mirror in the dressing room adjacent to her guest suite that was, she was sure, larger than the living room/dining room/kitchen area in her small apartment. "It's ugly."

"Your job here is not to choose garments that you might like to wear for a day in your life," Theo had replied, in that inexorable way of his that made her want to obey him, please him, almost as much as she wanted to run screaming from him. He had moved closer to her, once again standing behind her in the mirror.

"Because a day in my life would, of course, be like a fate worse than death," she'd said bitterly, pretending she hadn't noticed the heat of him, so near to her. That she'd been unaware of the way her breasts had felt fuller, her thighs looser, her skin hotter. She'd hated herself for that weakness.

"The point is to observe a dress like this and try to understand the art of its creation," he'd said softly, his gaze dark in the mirror, his head too close to hers, *much too close*. That glimmer in his eyes made her believe that he was not what he seemed, not just another Whitney family minion. "Larissa had an effortless sense of style. You will not have to dress yourself without help, of course, but understanding what drew her eye will help you understand *her*."

"All I understand," she'd said, her heart thumping too fast, her voice too thin, "is that rich people apparently have the time and the money to pick clothes to make statements rather than to serve a purpose. Like, for example, simply clothing themselves."

"They pick whole lives just to make statements," Theo had replied, his gaze clashing with hers, daring her to look away, yet snaring her in its amber grip. "Because they can."

"And by *they*, you mean *you*," she'd whispered, desperate to sound fierce yet fearing she sounded only pointlessly defiant.

A smile she'd have called *painful* were he someone else had crossed his dangerous mouth then, and his eyes had darkened. She'd thought she'd felt the faintest of touches on the back of her hair, as if he'd run his hand down the gleaming blond length of it. As if he was caressing a ghost.

"You are here to understand Larissa," he said quietly. "Not me. You should not try. I doubt you'd like what you find."

What did it mean that for a single moment, yearning and bittersweet, she had almost wanted to be Larissa for him?

She told herself that it was easier when he was off tending to his multitude of duties as CEO of Whitney Media, sequestered away in his home office that boasted its own elevator lobby and entrance, so that his endless succession of business meetings could take place without anyone any the wiser that a doppelganger sat right across the hall, learning how to be a bored, vapid socialite the world thought was locked away in a very private rehabilitation center, safe from prying eyes and tabloid articles.

Not that the lack of access to Larissa kept the tabloids from speculating about her very public collapse. They hired doctors who had never treated her to opine on her supposed course of treatment. They printed her greatest hits—a parade of embarrassing pictures under screaming headlines supposedly expressing concern—and made up sightings. Becca was almost tempted to feel some sort of sympathy for the poor girl. Almost.

She told herself that the long hours she was left to her own devices—expected to keep reading up on Larissa's highly pedigreed history so she could spout it off by rote, left to roam around Theo's stunning home like the ghost she sometimes wondered if she was becoming— were better. That being around him irritated her and infuriated her. And perhaps that was true, but she couldn't deny that her heart leaped when he returned to her. That she looked forward to it—and to the nights spent learning table manners fit for dining with royalty, nights filled with his endless corrections. How to stand, how to sit, how to laugh, how to appear politely indifferent. She found she looked forward to fencing words with him far, far more than she should. More than she was willing to admit, even to herself.

There was something in the darkness he carried within him and brandished like both shield and sword that called to her, much as she wanted to deny it. Something that agitated her, that stirred her blood and kept her awake late into the night, tossing and turning on a wide, luxurious bed that she could not seem to get comfortable in, ever. Something that seemed to call out to her, to sing in her, too, like a perfect harmony she'd been waiting to sing her whole life.

Don't be ridiculous, she told herself now, snapped back into the present morning on the terrace, with the faint sounds of angry rush hour horns and the inevitable sirens rising from the New York City streets far below. *The man is in love with his comatose fiancée. And you are showing worrying signs of Stockholm Syndrome.*

"So you do," she heard herself say, her mouth doing as it liked with no thought to the consequences. As if she would not have to pay the price for her foolishness.

"I do what?" He did not even look at her. *Tap tap tap* on the keyboard, nations his to command at will. His voice was completely dismissive, letting her know exactly where he ranked her in his estimation.

She had the passing thought that he seemed to go out of his way to do so, when she had only ever seen him treat his actual servants with a warmth and a respect that suggested he did not consider himself *quite* so lofty… but why should he treat her any differently? But she was still talking, apparently—still belaboring the point.

"Love her." She studied the side of his beautiful face, the elegant line of his jaw that was somehow wholly masculine, the rich black of his thick hair. "You love Larissa."

She told herself she did not shiver when his amber gaze, dark and measuring, met hers, a fire she could not understand building in those mesmerizing depths.

"She was my fiancée," he said in that clipped tone that she knew by now meant she should stop talking, that he was losing his temper. But she couldn't seem to do it. There was something swelling inside of her, rolling through her, that she couldn't understand. It made her want to poke at him, to prod at him, and she didn't even know why. Because she did not—could not—*want* this man, not like that. Not the way he clearly wanted his perfect princess, his lost Larissa.

"She had a lover, too," she said—suicidally. "What do you think he feels for her?"

Theo closed his laptop with a careful, gentle movement that was somehow more unnerving than if he'd slammed the screen shut. Becca swallowed, and let her grapefruit spoon clatter to her plate. What was the matter with her? Why was she determined to get under his skin? Was she that desperate to compete with a woman she'd never met, but who she saw more of in the mirror every day?

A cold sort of awareness swept over her, through her, then—making the hair on the back of her neck and along her arms stand on end.

"You'll have to ask him what he feels," Theo said in that mild way of his that sent every alarm in her body off in a wild cacophony of sound and panic. She felt herself straightening against her chair again, in unconscious defense, and couldn't bring herself to stop it even as she felt it happen. "But in my experience, Chip Van Housen has never loved anything, not even himself."

"You know him." It was a breath of sound, hardly speech at all.

Theo almost shrugged—a movement dismissive even of itself. "I've known him for years. He grew up in the same social circle with Larissa and has been a noted bad influence on her whenever possible." He did not sound the way Becca thought a man who'd been cheated on should sound. He was too calm. Too measured.

"How modern and forward-thinking of you to be so at ease with their relationship," she said, sniffing slightly, and then froze when he turned the full force of his gaze on her—his eyes so dark they were hardly amber at all. His mouth twisted, his body tensed, and she knew, suddenly, like a searing bolt of lightning through her heart, that this was the real Theo Markou Garcia. This was who he kept wrapped up beneath the polished exterior and the dizzying displays of wealth. This man—elemental and electric, raw and dangerous.

She should have been afraid. Terrified. But instead she felt...alive. Exhilarated. What did that make her? What did it mean? But she was afraid she knew.

"I am not the least bit modern," he bit out. His eyes flashed. "But I learned long ago how to pick my battles. You should do the same."

"This is ridiculous!" she cried several nights later, abruptly pushing away from the gleaming length of the dining room table.

Theo watched her as she rose, noticing the thrum of energy in her body, the roll of her hips—so suggestive, so impertinent—so very different from Larissa's boneless, bored-looking saunter. He could practically *see* frustration shimmer from Becca's skin, and could not help his own immediate reaction to her—she was like a live wire. He shifted in his chair.

"I have told you repeatedly—" he began, but she whirled back around to face him, magnificent in a floor-length gown in a deep, lush shade of chocolate. It made her skin seem to glow, highlighting the delicate lines of her face and her rich, full lips.

"You do nothing *but* tell me," she interrupted fiercely. "How to walk, how to stand. How to breathe. And I am having a delightful time playing Eliza Doolittle to your Henry Higgins, but this is too much."

"Dinner?" he asked dryly, eyeing her over the expanse of silver platters, all of them displaying food he knew was cooked to delectable perfection. She was breathing too hard, he thought. She was far too agitated. He wished that awareness of her did not move through him like a caress. "I will notify the chef of your displeasure."

"The food is perfect," she said with a sigh. "It always is. I'm sure you insist upon nothing less."

He did, of course, but he did not much care for the way she said that—as if that was yet one more flaw she had discovered in him. He did not know why it should matter to him if she'd found a thousand flaws. Why should anything she said or did affect him in the least? And yet it did. *She* did. More and more with every day, when he should view her as nothing but one more employee. He leaned back in his chair.

"We were having a conversation about local events and the theater," he said, making sure to sound as bored as he ought to feel, yet did not. "Hardly worth all this carrying on. You could simply have changed the subject if you'd become tired of it."

Some shadow seemed to move over her face, and when she looked at him, she seemed something very close to sad.

"What's the point of all this?" she asked. Her voice was softer, but there was still that great darkness in her eyes, belied by the sparkle of the sapphires at her throat, the glorious sweep of her bright hair against the dark windows behind her. "Why are you trying to turn me into a proper Victorian maiden? I think we both know that's not at all who Larissa was."

"Do we?" He found her spellbinding, and could not account for it. It was not that she looked so much like Larissa—though she did, and more with every moment—it was that the more she resembled her cousin, the more he could only seem to focus on the things that made her uniquely her.

She moved toward the table again, as if pulled by a force beyond her control. He felt the same way when he looked at her, but could not allow himself to act on it. She did not deserve to be dragged down in this madness, just as Larissa deserved more from him than this casual defection, this unexpected yearning for another woman when he had promised to be better than that. Better, by far, than she had ever been.

"You're acting as if Larissa was prim and proper," she said, her gaze flicking over his face as if looking for clues. "Is that what you think? Because she didn't collapse outside of that club by accident, Theo. And she's famous for her wild nights of partying, not her intimate, elegant dinner parties for eighteen."

He was distracted by the sound of his name in her mouth. Had she used it before? He wanted her to taste far more of him. And he hated himself for it.

"You don't know her," he said, his voice curt.

"Do you?" she asked, and it was worse that her tone was so even, so quiet. So thoughtful. "Or are you making me into your fantasy of who you think she should have been? Who you wanted her to be?"

That should not have surprised him as much as it did. It should not have cut into him, deep and fierce. She was too incisive, this ghost of his own creation; too intuitive. She saw too much. It was as if the formal dining room around them contracted, and there was only the way she looked at him, as if she knew all of his secrets—and it hurt her.

It made him want her all the more, despite everything.

"Does it matter?" he asked, fighting to keep his voice

even. "As long as you get what you want, why should you care what version of her I need you to play?"

She shook her head as if she fought back some harsh emotion, but he could not see why she should—she was the stranger here. She was the only one who would escape unscathed when all of this was over, while Theo would preside over the great bonfire of the hollow victory that would be his. All his, but without the greatest prize of all. But then, he knew better—he knew that even if Larissa had lived, even if she'd married him as she'd promised, she would never truly have been his. They'd ruined that possibility long ago.

"Isn't being a CEO enough?" she asked, as if she could not make sense of him. As if she wanted to. "Must you *own* the company, too?"

Theo was on his feet without knowing he meant to move, restlessly closing the space between them, his attention focused on her wary gaze, her resolute expression. Why did he want to touch her when he should want only to put her in her place? Why was he having so much trouble remembering what that place was?

"You have me all figured out, don't you?" He could not seem to stay an appropriate distance from her, as he knew he should. He felt drawn to her, by the shimmer of emotion in the air, by the shrewd intelligence in her hazel eyes. By the ache of all the things he could never have, not with this woman nor the one she so resembled. The things he'd sacrificed in service to his drive, his ambition. "You've judged me and delivered your sentence."

"Why can't you just leave the poor girl alone?" she asked, sounding very nearly desperate, but there was a huskiness to her voice that he knew was because he was near. He felt it, too—the surge of electricity, the dance of heat, that arced between them. He was much too close to forgetting why he should continue to ignore it. Betraying himself, betraying Larissa, betraying the promises he'd made and meant, he reached over and captured her slim, toned bicep in his hand. He felt the way she jumped at his touch, felt the way she shivered against his hand.

As if she saw him as a man. A real man. Not a convenient excuse or a bargaining chip in a never-ending battle against an overbearing father.

"Larissa is not who you think she is," he said softly, urgently, as if it was important for her to understand. As if it mattered. All the things he needed threatened to overwhelm him, to crack his control to pieces, and then what? She would still be a ghost. The reflection of the woman he'd never quite had, and wholly someone else, someone new, all at once.

Becca looked at his hand on her arm for a long moment, then slowly raised her hazel gaze to his.

"I know more about Larissa Page Whitney than I do about myself," she said. Her brows rose, challenging him. Beckoning him. "But nothing at all about you."

"I am sure you can read endless articles about me online," he said, letting his fingers test the smooth, bare flesh of her upper arm. Testing his limits. Testing her response. He angled himself closer, mesmerized by the way her lips parted, by the way her eyes gleamed with heat. "If you find yourself horribly bored and in need of some slight entertainment."

"I don't want to know about the CEO of Whitney Media," she whispered. "I want to know about *you*."

He was so close. He needed only to bend his head and he could taste her, finally. He could not remember a time he had not wanted her, desperately. *Her,* he thought. Not

Larissa. But how could that be, when Larissa had been the only thing he'd ever wanted, ever allowed himself to consider wanting—for ages now? When she had so long been the brass ring, just out of reach? Yet he could not seem to stop himself as he knew he should.

He pressed his lips against her cheek, tasting the silken softness of her skin. She was vanilla and cream, and the taste went straight to his sex. He ached. He forgot any woman but this one.

"Ask me anything," he said, his mouth so close to hers he thought he could already taste the drugging heat of her.

"Who are you kissing?" she asked, her voice a thread of sound, but seeming to pound through him like a drumbeat, loud and sure. As the words penetrated, he lifted his head, and her hazel eyes were too bright as they met his, but brave. "Her or me?"

CHAPTER FIVE

HE LOOKED AS IF SHE'D slapped him. She felt as if she had.

He stepped back, letting his hand drop from her arm. The stark contrast between his warm palm and the cool air of the dining room around them felt like a sudden punishment. Her cheek burned where he'd kissed her, and she felt that searing heat deep in her core. But she could not take back her question. She was not even sure she wanted to. She still could not figure out which sick part of her had asked it.

Or why she wanted so desperately to hear his answer.

He moved instead to the long table and picked up his wineglass, taking a long pull of the rich red liquid before setting it down, and Becca could not help but notice how easily he moved, how gracefully, even when she suspected he was as off balance as she was.

She was in deep trouble with this man. There was no use denying it. He had just tried to kiss a ghost and she...

It did not bear thinking about. She was not even sure what had come over her in the first place. They had been having dinner. It had been...far too *easy*. Fine wine, interesting conversation. She had been involved in what he was saying, even relaxing as she'd gazed at him in the gentle glow of the candelabra and the sparkling chandelier above. Maybe that very easiness was what had tipped her over the edge. The dizzy feeling that if she only squinted, if she only let go of herself completely, she could disappear completely into this fantasy world. She could really be the woman who had been meant to sit at this table, with this man. After all, she already looked just like her.

Maybe what had scared her was how little she thought she'd mind.

"I wanted only to use you because you look like her," he said finally. If he was another man, she might have thought him awkward. Unsure. But he was Theo, and he straightened and faced her, proud and unyielding. "I did not expect anything further than that—an elaborate ruse, perhaps, but just a ruse. I did not anticipate that I would want you."

"I don't think you do." It was so hard to say—but she shrugged when his flashing amber gaze slammed into hers. All that heat made her throb, then ache, then melt. She forced herself to breathe. To continue to say what must be said, or it might explode inside of her. "I think you want her. The more I look like her, the more you look at me. The more you long for her." She even smiled then, though it hurt more than it should. Far more than she was willing to admit to herself. "It makes sense. She's your fiancée and she's lost to you. It would be odd if you did not feel these things."

His jaw worked for a moment, and then he let out a small, mirthless laugh. It rang hollow through the vast room, like a kind of chill in the air itself.

"You don't know her," he said shortly. "You are talking about fantasies and feelings. Games. My relationship with Larissa was nothing like you imagine it to be."

"Why did you want to marry her?" she asked, shaking her head slightly. Why did she want—so desperately—to see things in him that weren't there, depths he did not possess? Why did it hurt her to imagine he was exactly who he claimed to be—and why did she want to convince him otherwise? Why did she imagine that she could see a different man inside of him? Her mouth felt dry. "Was it just a merger? A business transaction?"

It wasn't that she found it hard to believe, in theory. After all, she was nothing more than a *business transaction* herself. She certainly had no trouble envisioning her loathsome uncle championing exactly that kind of thing—it was Theo she couldn't imagine succumbing. Why should he marry anyone, for any reason aside from his own desire to do so?

His hard mouth crooked, and he thrust his hands into the pockets of his devastatingly elegant suit. It was the first time she had ever seen him anything even remotely approaching disheveled, and she found she was holding her breath.

"It was clear very early in my career at Whitney Media that I was headed for the top," he said with a certain matter-of-factness, completely devoid of ego and all the more powerful for its unvarnished honesty. "It was no secret that I wanted nothing less, and soon enough, I came to Bradford's attention. But Bradford prefers to keep the control of his family's company within the family." He gave her a cool look.

"So she was merely your bargaining chip." Becca tried to keep the disappointment from her voice, her expression. How had she convinced herself that a man like this had fallen in love? That he *could?* That he was different, somehow, from her uncle? How had she let herself believe it? He, like Bradford, wanted what he could conquer. He wanted what he viewed as his. How had she forgotten for even a moment the circumstances that had brought her here?

This was the man who had ordered her to spin around in front of him for his perusal. This was the man who had kept her from walking out of the Whitney mansion.

What *wasn't* this man capable of? And when had she lost sight of that?

"You mistake me yet again," Theo said in that deadly way of his, that made her shiver deep inside. She called it fear—though something in her knew better, even now. Even after all she'd learned. "She was never my bargaining chip. I was hers."

"I did not end up at Whitney Media by accident," Theo heard himself say, somewhat bemused by the fact he was speaking of this at all—of his past. It was something about the way Becca looked at him—as if she thought he owed her this explanation. But why did he seem to agree? "It did not simply *happen*. I fought to get here, every step of the way."

"So you did not, in fact, rise to power on the backs of the downtrodden?" Becca asked, those marvelous eyebrows arching high. "I thought that was the first step of any would-be mogul."

"I understand your anger," Theo said, eyeing her as if that would help him understand this uncharacteristic urge to unburden himself. "But my childhood was far more desperate than yours could ever have been."

"Should we compare notes?" she asked, a sting in her tone. "Should we see who suffered more?" She looked pointedly around her. "It seems pretty clear to me that one of us came out with a whole lot more."

"It is not a competition," he said in a low voice. He inclined his head. "But if it was, I would win."

He thought of the heat, the fear. The thick Florida nights his family had sweated through, huddled together in the dark with the lights off to avoid the roaming gangs, the guns, the ever-present violence of the streets.

"And here I assumed that you were one of them," she said, her hazel gaze traveling over him, from head to toe. She met his eyes and shrugged. "Prep school, summers on the Cape, rugby shirts and a golden retriever. The whole package." He would have thought she was being flippant, had he not seen that defensive, wounded look in her eyes. She hid it almost immediately, but he saw it. He recognized it.

She was not at all unlike him, this woman, and he did not know how to handle the rush of something like pleasure he felt when he thought it. He ignored it instead.

"Not quite." His smile felt thin. "My father dropped dead unexpectedly, leaving my mother to fend for herself in Miami, when his proud Cuban family had turned their backs on him for marrying a Greek Cypriot immigrant." He could hear his voice in the air between them, heavy with irony, ripe with old condemnation. When had he last talked of these things? Had he ever talked of these things? "We had nothing. No money. No hope. Less than you could possibly imagine."

He thought of his older brother Luis, gunned down on the street like garbage as payback for some imagined slight. He thought of his mother's face, twisted in agony, and the anguished fire in her eyes when she'd looked at him. *Not you, Theo,* she had whispered fiercely, her fingers digging into his narrow shoulders. He had been

barely eleven years old. *You will not die in this place.*
You will get out.

And so he had, one painful step at a time.

"I saw the Whitneys many years ago, when I was
young," he said, unable to look at Becca, suddenly. He
turned toward the great windows, but hardly noticed the
glittering spectacle of Manhattan arrayed before him,
sparkling and gleaming in the night. Instead he saw a
packed street in South Beach, outside one of the area's
most exclusive restaurants, teeming with vibrant people,
Latin music, the Miami high life. "Bradford and his wife
were visiting Miami with their perfect little daughter.
She could not have been ten. I was parking cars, and I
thought they all looked like movie stars, like a fantasy.
I thought she looked like a princess. And I wanted what
they had, whatever they had." He laughed shortly. "I
didn't know who they were until years later."

"It is hard for me to imagine Bradford looking perfect," Becca said, her voice crisp, cutting into his memories—making them seem somehow less horrific. Was
that her intent? How could it be? "Or anything even
approaching perfect, for that matter."

"That is because you are predisposed to find his kind
of power offensive," Theo replied. He did not to turn to
look at her—and in any case, he saw only himself as the
young teenager he had been, so captivated by Bradford's
ease and confidence. It had been so very different from
the kind of dead-eyed swagger that had meant power
and authority in his neighborhood. It had changed his
whole world. He let out a short laugh. "But I had never
seen it before. It was a revelation."

How could he describe his life to her, the way it had
been back then? When he thought of it, it was almost
as if it was someone else's life altogether. A movie he'd

once seen, perhaps, of a desperate young boy and all he'd done not only to escape his dead-end world, but to succeed by any measure. He had clawed his way out of that pit, inch by painful inch. How could he possibly explain what that had been like to this woman? She had never reached the heights he had, and he knew she had never been so low.

"When I was fresh out of business school I came to New York," he continued in a low voice, skipping over the indescribably hard years in between—the sacrifices and impossible feats he had made possible, somehow, because he'd had no other choice. And it had still meant nothing, in the end, despite his best efforts. He had been unable to save his mother from the cancer that had taken her, just as he'd been unable to save his brother back in Miami. "And Larissa was everywhere."

"Doing what?" she asked, her voice faintly dubious, as if she was imagining the kind of tabloid antics Larissa was famous for, and judging them harshly.

"Being Larissa," he said. He turned back then, to look at her. To see the face that had haunted him for so many years, from long before he'd actually met Larissa through to now, when she was irrevocably lost to him and yet was this new, other person, too. *Becca.* "She was always in the papers. She was always being photographed. She was one of the most recognizable faces in New York." He shrugged. "She was like a dream."

Becca reached over to run her hand along the back of one of the chairs at the table, and he had the distinct impression that she was choosing her words carefully.

"What kind of dream?" she asked finally, her tone a shade too polite.

He could not help but wonder what she had not said, what she'd hidden.

"I suppose you could say she was the emblem of all I ever wanted," Theo said after a moment. He could not help the sardonic laugh that escaped him at that little truth. What did it make him to have wanted Larissa so much and gotten so little in return? But he had made his peace with that long ago, he told himself. One did not fall in love with an emblem. Not really. One accepted her terms and displayed her in return, especially if one was far too busy with business to worry about his emotional life.

And it would have been different once they'd married. He was sure of it.

Despite everything, he still carried those first pictures of her in his head, as if he'd imprinted on them. Larissa caught in laughter on the glossy pages of a magazine, carefree and easy, so beautiful and so captivatingly, astonishingly perfect. A woman like that, he'd thought then, with her effortless beauty and her gleaming pedigree, would be the icing on the great and glorious cake he planned to make of his life, with his own hands. He had been determined to build his own empire—and a woman like that would be like a beacon to show all the world that he'd succeeded. That *he,* Theo Markou Garcia, who came from dirt and should never have managed to climb his way out, was the man with all the power.

"Your ultimate fantasy is a spoiled debutante?" Becca asked, her voice cool. "I can't blame you, I suppose." Her voice indicated that, in fact, she could. "Aren't all men predisposed to choose *vapid* over *interesting?*"

"Is this some form of envy?" he asked, studying her face, so like and yet unlike Larissa's. The more he looked at her, the less he saw Larissa at all. Particularly when he saw the flash of temper she hurried to conceal. "Do you think you would not be chosen?"

"Chosen for what?" she asked, laughing slightly, derisively. "To be some man's trophy, with no thought to who I might be as I am reduced to an *emblem?* Or chosen to play some elaborate game of pretend to benefit some man's lust for power?" Her mouth curved into something not quite a smile. "Thank you, but I'd pass. If I could."

There was something almost too painful in the space between them then, pulling taut, making him long to put his hands on her almost as much as he wanted to deny her words applied to him.

He could not name the fire she stirred in him. But he burned. Oh, how he burned.

"I knew that if I was ever in a position to win a woman like that, I would be exactly where I'd always wanted to be," he said finally. He did not understand his urge to explain himself to her. He had never spent any time at all concerned about the opinions of others. Why should he start now?

"Congratulations," Becca said, her eyes dark though her voice was light. "You got everything you wanted, didn't you? The woman you always wanted. And the whole company along with her."

"When I started at Whitney Media I announced in the very first training session that I would run the company one day," he said without meaning to speak, without knowing what he meant to say. "The HR manager laughed in my face. She was not laughing five years later."

"Five years?" Becca asked. "That's all it took?"

"I don't know how to lose," he said, because that

was the salient point. He wasn't bragging. He had never bragged. He didn't have to. "I have no other choice."

She didn't know why she found that statement, so simple and so matter-of-factly delivered, heartbreaking. Wasn't this his story of success? His rise to unimaginable heights? Shouldn't a story like this be accompanied by swelling music and a cheering section? Why, then, did she want to cry? To try to reach across the space between them and touch him somehow?

"But what exactly have you won?" she said softly. "The CEO, but without the shares you need to truly be an owner. Engaged to Larissa, but still alone."

His gaze hardened, and she thought she saw temper flex his jaw before he hid it behind that dark, arrogant mask.

"Careful," he suggested, in that deadly voice—the one that had ruined her so completely the day she'd met him. The one that made her tremble slightly even now. "It is one thing to share information that might help you in your portrayal. It is another to shoot your mouth off about things you can't possibly understand."

"What's to understand?" she asked lightly, as if completely unaware of the darkness in his tone, his gaze. "You are engaged yet don't live together. You have her things shipped here as you need them." She shrugged, as if she felt at all casual. "And somehow, I don't quite believe that Larissa, of all people, was saving herself for marriage."

Theo gazed at her now, his hard, devil's face set in lines that no longer intimidated her as much as they had at first. Instead, tonight, she wanted to trace them with her hands. She wanted to taste him, learn him, *know* him. But not if he thought she was someone else. Not while he wanted that someone else so desperately. She still had that much pride, at least.

For now, a treacherous voice whispered deep inside of her.

"It was never a conventional relationship," he said coldly. "How could it have been?"

"Why shouldn't it have been?" Becca asked, frowning.

"She could have chosen anyone," Theo said, his voice stiffening. But there was something else there, beneath his words. Something that made it sound as if he was the one who hadn't deserved the selfish, vain girl and her careless treatment. The very idea set Becca's teeth on edge. "But she chose me, and then, later, agreed to marry me when we decided it would be most beneficial. It was a bargaining chip in her endless war with her father, but she also knew that I understood her. I would wait for her to settle into the relationship. I would not force her into something she wasn't ready to accept."

"Like fidelity?" Becca asked dryly.

"She was not the woman I'd imagined her to be before I met her," Theo said, ignoring her. "But she was not the monster you imagine her to be, either." He sighed, and shook his head slightly. "Try to imagine her life."

Becca couldn't help the slight laugh that escaped her then. She could see her reflection in the grand mirror that dominated the far wall, and it was shockingly similar to the many pictures she'd seen of Larissa over the years. Dressed to kill, jewels to wound, with nothing more pressing on her plate than another charity event, another art opening, another party. Did Theo really think that Becca *hadn't* pored over those magazines? Hating herself for her own sick fascination with the life she might have had, the person she might have been?

"I've imagined her life more times than I can count," Becca said now, fighting to keep her voice smooth, even. To keep the years of anger at the injustice of it all at bay. "I imagined what I could do with her money, how I might appreciate the vacations and clothes and parties and opportunities that bored her so terribly. Is that what you want me to imagine?"

"It can't have escaped your notice that Bradford Whitney is the last person on earth anyone would want as a father," Theo said coldly, as if he'd judged her for her callousness. She wished she didn't care. She *wanted* not to care. "He drove Larissa's poor, fragile mother to a nervous breakdown. She never leaves the house in France anymore. She's become a complete recluse."

"Again," Becca said evenly, refusing to back down from that condemning look he shot at her, "what would you like me to imagine? What it's like to have a bad father? I have one of those. The moment my mother was thrown out of the Whitney family, my father disappeared. But my mother couldn't swan off to a house in France to recover. She had to figure out how to be a single mother all on her own."

"Imagine what it must have been like for her, to grow up in that house, with those parents," Theo replied, hammering his point even further. As if she hadn't spoken. As if, Becca thought, he *needed* her to see Larissa as he wanted to see her. "She was never strong like you. She never had a chance."

"She had every chance," Becca retorted. She could feel her face heating, and knew she was saying too much. *Feeling* too much. Was she innately, naturally strong or had she simply never been given the option to be anything but? "More chances than most people can dream of!"

"She had money," Theo said, shaking his head. "That's not quite the same thing."

"How can you have grown up where you did, the way you did, and sympathize with a poor little rich girl like her?" Becca asked, unable to hold her emotions back. She felt it all flood into her, making her voice too loud and her eyes too bright. How could he defend a woman who had, from all accounts including his own, treated him like he was something too far beneath her to be worthy of her notice?

"Rich doesn't mean happy," he began.

"But it does mean *rich*," Becca threw at him, furious. At him. At Larissa, damn her. At this situation that was spiraling out of control with every word she couldn't seem to keep inside of her. "She had every advantage in the world. Literally."

"She is the saddest girl I've ever met," he said, his amber gaze slamming into her, making her heart stop, then pound.

As if he'd hit her.

"Are you talking about her *emotional pain?*" she asked, aware that her voice was no more than a whisper, barely audible, and yet it scorched her own throat. So scathing. So bitter. "Do you know who has time for emotional pain, Theo? Women like Larissa, who never have to worry about anything else. Not where her next meal is coming from. Not how she's going to pay the rent."

"You don't know her," he said again, his voice clipped.

"I wonder if you do," she threw at him. "You're so busy making excuses for her—you've even brought me here to pretend to be her because she betrayed you in yet one more way, and you still want to defend her."

"I won't listen to this—"

"You wanted me to study her, and I have," Becca said, throwing her words out like blows. Wishing they were. Wanting them to land, to hurt. Wanting him to wake up and see the truth—*needing* him to—though she refused to examine why. She kept on. "The woman you're carrying around in your mind doesn't exist, Theo. She never did."

"You forget yourself." His voice could have shattered steel. She felt a chill sneak along her neck, her arms, leaving goose bumps in its wake, and she knew she'd pushed him too far. His eyes bored into hers, amber turned glacial.

"Theo…" But he was no longer listening.

"You are the ghost in this room," he told her, in his most lethal tone, making her grip the chair in front of her to remain upright. "You're the one playing a part. You only exist insofar as I say you do."

His face was carved of stone, absent of light. It should have done her serious damage. Instead, she ached for him.

"I suggest you remember your place," he threw at her, and then he brushed past her and left her standing there, trembling and alone. And as pale as the ghost he'd accused her of being.

CHAPTER SIX

BECCA WOKE THE next morning feeling unaccountably fragile.

She moved slowly, sitting up and pushing her hair back from her face carefully, as if suffering from some kind of emotional hangover. Gingerly, she made her way into the vast, luxurious shower that had at first seemed shockingly lush and that she was now already far too comfortable using. She stood under the hot spray for a long, long time, willing the odd tilt and whirl of her feelings away.

Because this was Theo's world, a carafe of hot coffee waited for her in the elegant blue-and-white bedroom when she walked back into it. She poured herself a mug of the rich, nearly decadent brew, and took several bracing sips before she completed the final step of her morning ritual in this bizarre place and allowed herself to look in the mirror.

Where she saw only Larissa looking back.

She blinked, and saw herself again—and then had to put her hand against her abdomen to ease the knot of panic there away.

Things had gotten far too confused, she thought then, fighting off the odd sense of something like vertigo. It was all too messy, somehow. She was a stranger with her own face. How could that be anything *but* a mess? But she could change it, surely.

Just because that arrogant man thought he got to decide if she *existed* or not didn't make it true, she reminded herself fiercely, shaking off all the echoes of her illegitimate childhood, all of Bradford's harsh words, that Theo's comments last night had dredged up. It meant only that he was even more full of himself than she'd previously believed.

And if a hollow ache seemed to gape open behind her ribs and then bloom in the pit of her stomach, well, no one had to know that but her. And she was getting very, very good at burying the things she didn't want to think about, she thought wryly. Far too good, in fact.

She checked in with Emily quickly, making sure her sister was doing well even as she hurried off the phone—too conscious of the lies she had to tell to linger. But hearing her sister's voice was like a much-needed wake-up call. She would pack these unwanted emotions away and concentrate on the job at hand. On her purpose for being here—which was not to figure out the mysteries of Larissa or, more to the point, of Theo Markou Garcia. It didn't matter how intriguing he was, how her body hummed to life at the very thought of his hard mouth, his strong hands. She had to play a part, that was all. Then she would collect her mother's inheritance—Emily's future—and leave this empty, shiny life exactly as she'd found it. She would be happy to be rid of it.

That was the plan. That had always been the plan. She should feel happier about it, surely.

She dressed slowly, pulling together the kind of fashionable outfit that she imagined Larissa might wear. She chose a flirty little scarlet dress and a pair of boots, then fashioned her hair in a Larissa-esque slicked-back ponytail, low on her neck. She then sat down at the vanity table and began the laborious process of applying the kind of makeup women like Larissa, apparently, viewed as the bare essentials for everyday wear. She had to live under the expectation that she might be photographed at any moment, she reminded herself, an echo of Theo's lecturing tone ringing in her head. She had to learn that only in her private bedroom could she drop her defenses and be something other than public property.

Normally, Becca hated every moment of the process. She'd liked a bit of mascara and some judicious eyeliner now and then when she'd been back in her own life, but she'd always erred on the side of *practical* rather than *pretty*. Larissa's seventeen coats of this followed by a dusting of that seemed absurdly excessive to her. But today she found that she was almost grateful for the excuse. For the ability to put on a mask, layer by layer. Coat by coat.

Because last night had left her feeling much too raw, far too exposed. She didn't want to feel anything even approaching vulnerable. She wanted to lock the soft parts of herself away, because she had to concentrate on her endgame—on Emily—if she was going to make it through this.

It didn't matter how fascinating he was. It couldn't.

She had to find a way to remember that.

Theo was all business when she found him again, behind his massive desk in the office suite of the penthouse. He barely spared her a glance when she walked in, and even turned his high leather seat around toward the window to continue his phone conversation. She heard the terms *market share* and *network overhead,* and tuned out.

She wondered if he made everyone stand there, like a supplicant, waiting for the great gift of his attention. Why wouldn't he? Hadn't he told her last night to remember her place? This was a naked display of power. He was too busy to deal with her the moment she arrived—though the housekeeper had told her to go to his office—and yet she was too insignificant to be kept separated from his conversation. She was meant to feel more and more uncomfortable as she stood there, ignored.

It was shocking to think that he'd *learned* tricks like this, that they hadn't been genetically bestowed upon him at birth. Everything about him shouted out his dominance, his masculine arrogance, his mastery of himself and everything around him. Becca found she couldn't imagine him as a young boy, desperate to acquire even some small part of what was now his. In her mind, he must always have been this way. Larger than life.

"I trust you are not as sentimental today as you were last night," he said coldly, snapping her attention back to the present. He replaced the phone in its cradle and eyed her from across the wide expanse of his gleaming black desk.

Becca stiffened. "Are you?" she replied. When his dangerous brows arched, she sniffed. "Or is it not *my place* to ask such questions?"

She could feel the tension in the room skyrocket. It clenched a hard hand around her, like a fist, and squeezed tight, and she knew he must feel it, too, though he did not move so much as a muscle. His eyes somehow got *more* amber; lit up from within, temper and heat and something much darker she could not name.

Though it took her breath.

"I think you have Larissa's appearance well in hand,"

he said after a moment, as if she had not spoken at all. His gaze flicked over her, and she took the absence of criticism to mean approval.

How sad you are, she told herself when she realized she actually felt a little glow go through her at the thought of his approval. As if that was the Holy Grail.

"Is that how you play this game?" she asked quietly, clamping down on her anger—at herself most of all. "You will simply pretend not to hear me as it suits you?"

"If you are planning to throw a childish tantrum," he said in his dark, commanding way, making her flush too hot and feel that warmth sear the back of her eyes—was she so eager to please him? "Please let me know now, so I do not pointlessly rearrange my schedule."

"Heaven forfend," she murmured. She glared at him with all the force she could manage, which, unsurprisingly, had no noticeable effect on him at all. "It's not as if I've given up weeks of my life, and rearranged everything. Why should you be inconvenienced?"

He gazed at her, and this time, even though she knew it was deliberate and that he *intended* for her to feel foolish and small, she had to bite down on the inside of her cheek to keep from squirming. But she could do nothing about the way she flushed yet again, or the creep of that red heat across her face and down her chest.

And even then, , there was still that part of her that wanted nothing more than to reach out and touch him.

Damn him.

"If you're finished," he said, so calmly. So coolly. "I think it's time for a field experiment."

Theo studied her in the flattering light that spilled through the floor-to-ceiling windows, bathing the trendy

SoHo restaurant in afternoon sunshine. She looked radiant. Beautiful, serene.

And she was driving him slowly insane.

He had lost sleep over this woman, an occurrence so rare that he had not allowed himself to admit it was possible until he found himself standing at his window in the dark of night, drinking whiskey and brooding. And thinking only of the way she'd argued with him—the way she'd looked at him as if she hurt *for* him.

He could not seem to wrap his head around that. He could not make sense of it.

He no longer knew what he saw when he looked at her. It had all become tangled. Knotted and snarled beyond any possible redemption. He had shared things with her he'd never shared with anyone, and he'd tried to slap her back down when it had all become too much—and none of it had helped. And yet he found himself mesmerized by the way she held the heavy silverware in her delicate hands, the way she sneaked glances around her when she thought he wasn't looking. And why shouldn't she? This was the restaurant of the moment. Had Theo cared to, he could no doubt have identified most of the other patrons packing the place, as they all had to be very famous, very wealthy, or both, to get in at all.

What was this childish part of him that wanted her to know that? Wasn't it enough that *he* knew it?

He had no idea what was happening to him.

"Tell me about your childhood," he heard himself ask, breaking the silence between them. He toyed with his glass, and could not seem to breathe when she licked her full lips. Was that an indication of her nerves? Or this same fire that burned in him? He decided he didn't care. Nothing mattered but this lunch, this woman, this moment. Surely.

"Is that an order?" she asked, that challenging look on her face.

"Merely a request." But he smiled slightly, because she never quit, this woman.

"I hesitate to make myself more human in your eyes," she continued crisply, cutting into her steak with a certain deliberate precision that he suspected was the only outward sign of her temper, aside from her tone of voice. "That might make me *exist* independent of your permission to do so, and then where would we be?"

His smile deepened. "The futility of the fight never seems to faze you," he murmured, as much to himself as to her. She was his very own Don Quixote, tilting wildly at any windmill that caught her attention, and he could not help but admire her passion. Her foolish courage.

She put down her silverware with a *thunk* and met his gaze. Hers was that color between brown and green, and it called to him. So serious. So sincere. So unreasonably brave.

"Whereas you try to dominate everything you come into contact with," she countered. "Whether you need to prove something or not."

"You make me sound like a stray dog, humping your leg," he said dryly. Her eyebrows rose, and she did not refute it. He laughed then, throwing his head back and letting it pour from him—because she was right. Something about this woman made him feel reckless and untried. As if he had to prove himself. No wonder he was acting like a fool. When he looked at her again, her bright eyes looked almost dazed.

"I didn't know you were capable of laughter," she said, clearing her throat. She looked away, then back at him with her cool mask back in place. "I thought it was all gloom and ghosts with you."

"You don't know me very well," he said. He leaned forward, and idly picked up her hand, sliding his palm against hers, reveling in the contact. "But I assure you, I have better technique than a randy dog."

She pulled her hand away, but not before he felt her tremble, and saw the heat bloom in her cheeks, in her gaze.

"I'll have to take your word on it," she said primly. He sat back in his seat and she watched him warily for a moment. "Why this change of heart?" she asked. "Last night you were in a high temper, and now you want to know about my childhood? Why?"

"There is no reason we can't be friendly, Rebecca," he said, his voice low. Insinuating. He hadn't meant to sound as if he meant to seduce her...had he?

"There is every reason," she said, her voice husky though he could see how she fought it—it was written across her face. She sat straighter in her chair. "For one thing, the fact that you keep calling me by the wrong name. It's *Becca,* not *Re*-becca."

"Becca is a nickname for Rebecca," he replied, shrugging.

"It is," she agreed, smiling tightly. "If your name happens to be Rebecca. But my mother named me Becca. *B-E-C-C-A.* No nickname. No longer name. Just Becca." She tilted her head slightly as she looked at him. "Is that part of how you assert control? Play your little dominance games? You don't like someone's name so you change it—and they're too afraid of you to complain?"

"I hear no fear at all, but a great deal of complaint," he pointed out, still lounging across from her, almost idly. "This tactic cannot be very successful, can it?"

She pressed her lips together, then dropped her hands

into her lap. He imagined he could feel the table move, as if her knee was bouncing in its usual agitation, and then it stopped—as if she'd slapped it down with the hands he couldn't see.

"What is the point of this?" she asked, finally. "You don't care about my childhood, and you didn't bring me here, to a restaurant like this, to be *friendly*. You have an ulterior motive. You always do."

There was accusation and something else in her voice, something that tugged at him even as it hung between them for a moment, dancing in the bright sunshine yet just out of sight.

"Why must it be one or the other?" he asked, almost forgetting himself.

She smiled. It was a sharp-honed weapon, hardly a smile at all. "Because that's how you operate," she said. She glanced around her, flipping her sleek ponytail back over her shoulder. "I suppose this is a decent test run. What did you call it—a *field experiment?*" She frowned slightly as her gaze swept the crowded restaurant. "I've already seen at least five people take pictures of me—of us—with their cell phones. I assume that's what you wanted." Her voice dropped and she swayed forward, revealing her perfect cleavage and the hollow between them. "Larissa Whitney and her long-suffering fiance at a quiet, uneventful lunch, just like normal people."

He could not deny a single thing she'd said, and yet some part of him wished he could. That there were no ulterior motives at all. That they were simply two people at lunch, learning about each other. Why did he yearn for that with parts of himself he hardly recognized?

"Can't I enjoy an afternoon with a beautiful woman?" he asked softly. "Can't I get to know her?"

"No," she said, low and sure. Fierce. "*You* can't."

He wanted to protest. He wanted to truly forget everything but this moment, this crippling need that raged through him—but he could not quite do that. Not after everything he'd given up to get here. Not now. "Why not?" he asked instead.

"Because my only value to you is my resemblance to someone else," she said very deliberately, very calmly. Too calmly. "Therefore, my personal information is mine. You don't get access to it. You don't get to know me when what you're really after is her."

He had spent years planning to run Whitney Media, and then, in due time, to own it. He had focused on nothing but that singular goal, casting everything else aside in pursuit of it. Larissa had liked him when he was her rough-edged lover calculated to irritate her father; she had lost interest in him when he became more of a Whitney than the Whitneys themselves. But even so, they had hammered out their devil's bargain, their sad little dance toward Theo's lifelong dream. And he was so close to achieving that dream—the dream that had meant everything to him for almost as long as he allowed himself to remember, last night's trip down memory lane notwithstanding. He was *so close*.

And yet he looked across the small table and the city outside faded away, the bustle and chatter of the Manhattan hot spot disappeared, and all he could see was Becca. Her mysterious gaze, like the secret, shaded hollows of some cool, forgotten forest. The intelligence and the challenge. The invitation he was not even sure she knew she was broadcasting. But he knew. He could feel it throughout his body, hardening him, readying him, making his need for her burn like a wildfire through his limbs.

He could not seem to help himself. He looked at

her and wanted *more,* more than he'd thought himself capable of before. More than he'd had.

"And what if I want you?" he asked, as if he was a free man. As if he was someone else. As if she'd been the dream all along. "Just you. What then?"

CHAPTER SEVEN

HEAT LIGHTNING CRACKLED between them, making Becca's nipples pull tight. A low, insistent ache bloomed between her legs. She felt heat flood her face, and something too bright, too hot to be tears sear through her eyes.

She did not even know if she was breathing.

And Theo only lounged there, so close and yet separated by the fancy table and the fussy centerpiece, his gaze hard on her, like a fierce caress. She had the sudden sense that he was far more primitive than his elegant suit and carefully manicured appearance might suggest. She could suddenly *see* him, deep into him, as if somewhere inside they were the same—a matched set. She could *see* all the wildness and passion and heat that burned in him, and burned in her, too.

How could she want him like this? A bone-deep longing crashed over her then, moving through her like the rising tide, making her whole body, every cell and every stretch of her skin, *yearn.*

But they were in public, this was all a charade, and she would never really know *who* he was looking at that way, would she?

It made her heart hurt. She reached up as if to cover it with her hand before she knew what she meant to do. Her palm flexed below her collarbone before she dropped it back in her lap.

"You don't," she said. She meant to sound strong. Dismissive. But instead, her voice got tangled in her throat, and it was only a whisper. "You don't want me."

"Don't I?"

"Of course not." She tore her gaze from his, and looked down at her plate, scowling fiercely to stem the panic, the emotion, the threat of tears. "You want whatever you've been carrying around in your head all these years. I'm the captive audience as well as the show. That's what you want, not me."

"I want to know how you taste," he said, his voice like a drug, narcotic and thrilling, moving over her like his mouth had last night, spinning out fires in every direction, though he did not move. He did not need to move. "Your neck. That hollow between your breasts. I want to taste every inch of you. And then start again."

She could not breathe. She could not look at him. She was paralyzed—as afraid of what he might say next as she was terrified that he would stop speaking. How could she be so conflicted? Why did he torment her so much? She had never had any trouble with men, and she had thought that all her coworkers' talk of theatrics and fireworks and life-altering complications were just the stories people told themselves, the way they brightened things up, as real as their claims that they would join the Peace Corps, write that book, or pack up and move to Fiji someday.

But now she knew better. Now she *knew*. She'd been waiting for Theo to incinerate her. Her whole life she'd waited, and now she burned, and he was in love with a woman he could never have—a woman Becca could never be, no matter what she looked like. It might not be her idea of love—it might make her angry to think it was what he thought he deserved—but none of this was within her control, was it?

"I want to move inside of you until the only thing you know, the only thing you can say, is my name," he continued, unaware, perhaps, of what he was doing to her with just those silky, disturbing, sensual words. Or all too aware it.

"Stop," she said then, her voice much weaker than it should have been. Almost as if she was pleading with him. "We're in public. People are watching."

"You should feel safe, then," he said, so arrogant. So offhandedly powerful. So at peace with the sensual danger that thickened in the breathing space between them. "What can happen here, with all of New York looking on?"

"What about your plan?" she threw at him, desperate, even as her breasts seemed to swell and she felt very nearly feverish, hot and then cold. "Is this how you and Larissa acted in restaurants?"

The name was like a slap of cold water. She could see the way it worked on Theo, reminding him. Changing him.

She had thrown the name out there deliberately. So she should not have felt so...betrayed by the way he reacted. So hurt.

"You have already achieved what I wanted today," he said, all that electricity slipping behind his smooth, corporate mask. Though his eyes still burned, still bored deep into her and stirred her in ways that should not thrill her as they did. "You have been seen in public, all in one piece. No one has looked at you as if you are anything but what and who you appear to be."

"Wonderful," Becca said tightly.

He surprised her then, by leaning forward and taking her hand in his again, this time gently holding on when she tried to pull it away. His skin against hers. The heat of him, exploding into her palm, sending shock waves up her arm and into her breasts, her belly.

"But you and I both know what lies beneath the surface," he said, in that snake charmer's voice, smoky and low, while his amber eyes made promises that left her aching all over. For him. For things she dared not even think through.

"I already told you," she gritted out. "You don't know me, and you won't. That's not part of the deal."

"I know you." His gaze dropped to their linked hands, and she was sure she could feel the heat of it, scorching her, leaving marks on her skin. "You are prickly and full of pride. Qualities I recognize and even admire. You've sacrificed yourself for your sister, no doubt your mother, too."

"My mother—" she began fiercely.

"Made her own choices," he interrupted smoothly. With perfect confidence that she would fall silent, and she did, not even hating herself for that acquiescence as she thought she should. As she knew she would later. "But still, you feel guilty. And so you are here, an angry hen set down amongst the foxes, to get what should have been yours by birth."

"You are a randy dog and I am a chicken," she said dryly. "What other residents of the barnyard will we be before this is over, I wonder?"

"You use this attitude and your wit as a shield," he continued as if she had not spoken. "And sometimes as a weapon. You attack before you can be attacked. And you do not back down, even when you must know you should. Sometimes retreat is a strategy, Becca."

"Then feel free to employ it," she snapped at him. She wanted to squirm in her seat. She wanted to yank back her hand, leap to her feet and bolt for the door. She could lose herself in the city within moments. She could be back in Boston by evening. She and Emily would figure something out. They always did.

But she didn't move.

"And you are as fascinated by me as I am by you," he said then, his fingers tracing patterns against hers, his amber eyes pinning her, paralyzing her—reading into her, seeing truths that she knew she'd never be able to take back.

"Don't flatter yourself," she whispered, but she didn't pull her hand from his. She didn't look away. And she thought her heart was beating so loud that it might drown out the restaurant all around them. The city beyond. The planet.

"I don't have to flatter myself," he said softly. Intently. "I have only to look at you."

And see who? that cold, suspicious, *rational* part of her brain hissed. And that easily, it broke the spell. Becca yanked her hand from his as if she'd suddenly found it on a red-hot burner. She sat as far back in her chair as she could, though it was not nearly enough space. He seemed so big. As if he was the whole world.

"My mother had no idea how to take care of herself, much less a baby," she said abruptly, throwing her words out like a lifeline. Theo only watched her. *Waiting,* that small voice warned her. *Lying in wait.* But she could not stop talking. There was that reckless part of her that thought she saw more in him—that thought she saw *him.* "She found men who helped, in one form or another.

Though how helpful any of them were is really open to interpretation." She sucked in a breath. "Eventually we settled in Boston, where she actually married Emily's father. He was nice enough. Unless he was drinking."

Theo shifted in his chair, and Becca found her gaze drawn, inexorably, to the hard muscles in his chest, his toned torso. He was too beautiful. Too lethal. She should not play with fire, not with him. That way lay only ash and regret.

"So eventually she kicked him out and it was just the three of us. We did the best we could." She shrugged, feeling panicked and resentful suddenly—as if he had forced her to say those things, as if she had not simply offered them up because of the emotional currents between them that she was afraid to examine more closely. "Is that what you wanted to hear? My idyllic, illegitimate youth?"

"So defensive," he observed. Was that sympathy she saw move through his hypnotic eyes? Or worse—pity? She found the thought unbearable. "You have nothing to be ashamed of."

"I know that!" Her temper flared, and all those old wounds, scarred over with years of guilt, seemed to hurt all over again. Like they were new. "But my mother was ashamed anyway. She'd had bigger, better plans for herself. And for her daughters. I think that if she'd lived, she would have come to Bradford herself." She shook her head, and then glared at him. "And she didn't happen to conveniently resemble anyone. So she would have humiliated herself in front of that little toad of a man, *her brother,* and he would have sneered at her and sent her away. Just because he could."

That lay there between them for a moment, as heavy as the centerpiece. Becca couldn't understand why she'd said that in the first place and why, having said it and knowing it all to be true, she felt as if she'd gone too far. As if she'd blamed Theo unfairly for Bradford's theoretical behavior. What was the matter with her? If Theo wasn't guilty of this particular thing, that didn't mean he was blameless. After all, she was only here because of his Machiavellian little plan, wasn't she?

"You're probably right," Theo said after a moment, in that relentlessly unsentimental way of his. She should have found it brutal. Instead, oddly, she found his honesty far more soothing than any platitudes might have been. "But the fact that Bradford is not much of a human being should hardly matter to you," he continued. "Why should you care?"

"It doesn't," she said, though it did. "I don't."

But she had said too much, she realized, as a new silence fell between them, and Theo gestured imperiously for the check. She had said too much, revealed too much, and now she was in exactly the position she had resolved to avoid. He didn't deserve to know a damned thing about her. He didn't deserve anything save what he'd paid for.

So why, knowing that, had she opened herself up anyway?

Becca still hadn't answered that question to her own satisfaction when they arrived back at Theo's private Manhattan castle. They'd spent the ride back from the restaurant in silence; Theo stretched out in the limo's expansive backseat tapping away on his BlackBerry while Becca pretended to gaze out the window at the frenetic crowds on the city streets. In truth, she was obsessively going over every detail of their lunch in her head. She couldn't help but feel that everything had shifted between them, beneath her feet. That between last night's series of revelations and today's unbearable heat, the geography of their arrangement had remade itself. She just couldn't seem to figure out the map. Or if she'd ceded too much ground without realizing it.

The car glided to a smooth stop at the curb, and Becca jolted in her seat when Theo laid his big, warm hand on her arm.

When she raised her gaze to his, there was amusement in those amber depths. And the same electricity she felt in a white-hot current just beneath her skin. Yet when he spoke, his voice was cool.

"The paparazzi are here," he said. He inclined his head toward the sidewalk outside the car window, though his eyes never left hers. "Are you ready?"

"How can I possibly know if I'm ready?" she asked with perfect, baffled honesty, blinking. Could anyone be ready for that kind of intrusion? She looked out the thankfully tinted window, swallowing nervously when she saw the scrum of shady-looking men already jostling for position outside the car—already snapping pictures and shouting. One even slapped his hand against the car itself.

"They want a reaction," Theo said, his voice even. Calm. She jerked her attention away from the chaos in the street and back to him. "The more emotional you are, the better. They will say anything to goad you into the reaction they want. *Anything.* Do you understand?"

He was so at ease. So unperturbed that there were jackals baying out his name, separated from them by only a flimsy bit of steel and tinted glass. Becca felt the panicked fluttering of her heart slow as she looked at him. He was so…*solid.* So sure. As if he could save them both, by the sheer force of his will. As if he were the anchor in rough seas, and she needed only to hold on to him.

He wants *this particular storm,* she reminded herself. *He probably called these awful men himself!*

But that knowledge didn't change the fact that when he looked at her like that, as if he knew she was capable of whatever lay before her, she felt as strong as he believed her to be. As if she could do anything at all. Even run this gauntlet.

For him, a different, treacherous voice whispered, and she was so far gone she did not even shudder in horror. She only ignored it. And forced herself to smile.

"How bad can it be?" she asked lightly. She shook her ponytail back over her shoulder. "No matter what they say, they won't be talking about me, will they?"

How many times had he watched Larissa navigate these baying hounds? How many times had he marveled—sometimes with more cynicism than admiration, it was true—at her seemingly innate ability to use this kind of attention to serve her purposes, to send the messages she wanted to send or cause the exact sort of commotion she wanted to cause? How many times had he dealt with them himself, and regretted only that *dealing with them* meant giving them some kind of legitimacy?

The Whitneys lived in an endless media glare. The great American celebrity fishbowl. Theo had never questioned that. He had only learned what he could about it, and used that knowledge to his advantage. Larissa had never had to learn it—she had been brought up in it, She had courted the attention she received, and, he'd eventually realized, used the narratives the press spun about her as shorthand for her own life, until it was sometimes uncertain where *the press* ended and

Larissa began. He had known this, and still, he had merely watched his fiancée perform the intricate steps of this peculiar dance. He had never interfered, not even when they turned on her. Not even when they turned on him, too.

And yet *this* time, with this woman, he nearly lost his cool. *This* time he wanted to rend them apart, these squalid little men with their sordid insinuations. He wanted to break the arm of the man who dared shove against Becca as she moved past him, ducking against the driver's burly frame and outstretched arm, her face concealed behind big, dark sunglasses.

Theo was used to them—hell, he expected them, and even on occasion utilized them, like today. And yet he wanted to have them all thrown in jail for trespassing, for assault, for *something*—because he could see how difficult an ordeal the short walk from the car was for Becca. How her breath caught in her throat in panicked little gasps, how her body swayed every time they shouted Larissa's name. How she looked as if they were physically attacking her. But they were immune to any reprisals, these cockroaches, and Becca was stronger than she should have been. More warrior than woman, he thought. Quixote to the end. She simply kept walking. And the scum were forced to stop at the door to the apartment building, where the staff of doormen stood ready to do battle to keep them from the premises.

Theo found that he was holding on to his temper by the barest thread.

"I would have saved you from that if I could," he said quietly, taking her by the arm and steering her toward his private elevator. He could not read her gaze behind those sunglasses, but he could see the turn of her mouth, the faint quiver of her lower lip. And yet she stood too straight, too tall. As if she dared not bend, lest she break apart.

"But that would have defeated the purpose of taking me out to lunch," she said, her voice devoid of inflection. Of emotion. Of *Becca.* "So what would be the point?"

He said her name as the heavy doors slid closed behind them, enclosing them in the lush maroon-and-gold elevator car. But it was too quiet, suddenly, too close, and she was still standing there like a soldier.

"I had no idea that was what it felt like," she continued in that same empty voice. "All those cameras. All those *people.* So many of them, and so close." She squared her shoulders, in a show of bravery that seemed to roll through him, leaving marks.

"Becca," he said again, but she wasn't listening to him.

"But this is what you wanted, isn't it?" She slid her sunglasses up over her forehead and into her hair, and fixed him with those mossy-green eyes, so serious now, so dark. "I assume that's why you didn't prepare me. So I wouldn't look confident, or used to them. So I would look fragile instead. Like someone just recovered from a collapse and fresh from private rehab somewhere should look."

He had never hated himself more than he did at that moment. She was not even condemning him—which made it that much worse. She was simply accepting his ulterior motives, and he could not pretend that they weren't true. That he hadn't had exactly that thought, that hope. That he hadn't set the scene with exactly that end in mind.

What did that make him? He almost laughed at himself then—*make* him? This was clearly who he already was. Who he'd been for some time. What that meant, he wasn't at all sure he wanted to know.

"Becca," he said again, his voice unusually thick—as if it belonged to someone else. "I'm—"

"Don't you dare apologize!" she snapped at him, some kind of temper flaring in her—but at least that was better than the blankness. "This was the deal. This is the job. Did I say I couldn't handle it?"

"I didn't know you," he said, urgently, not meaning to move closer to her, not meaning to take her shoulders in his hands, not meaning to draw her into him, so her head tilted back and she looked up at him with those damned eyes of hers, that seemed to turn him into a stranger to himself. "I didn't know you at all. I only knew that you looked like her. I had no idea that this would be anything but a game for you to play."

She looked at him, and he had the uncomfortable sense that she saw things he didn't even realize were there. Something dark passed over her face, and when she smiled, it was brittle.

"Who says that it's not?" she asked. "It turns out that I'm good at passing for a spoiled little princess. Who could have guessed?" She laughed, a little bit wildly. "It must be those Whitney genes, after all."

"Don't do this," he said then, that urgency moving through him, making his voice rougher than it should have been.

"I don't understand," she said, her own voice uneven in return, the wildness fading from her expression, and something far older, far sadder, taking its place. "Is it that you don't want me to play this game according to the rules you set up yourself? Or is it that you don't want me to be any good at it?"

He found himself shaking his head, found his fingers

testing her toned muscles, found himself achingly, shockingly hard. He wanted to answer her with his body. He wanted to lose them both in the only truth that mattered to him right then. The only thing that could set them both free of a game he no longer understood the way he'd thought he would.

"I don't know," he said, with brutal honesty. He wanted things he couldn't name. He *wanted*. And she was Becca, not Larissa, and he couldn't seem to find that anything but perfect. Right. And her eyes held all the secret depths of the forest. And he wanted her, most of all. Now. But more than that, he wanted to be the kind of man who never would have hurt her, and it was already much too late.

Electricity seemed to hum in the air, and he could see only her. Only her, and that wild, unmanageable heat that only she seemed to stir in him, reflecting back at him. And then she sighed slightly, and he saw something almost like hopelessness flash in her gaze. But then she blinked, and it was gone.

She smiled then, heartbreaking and real, and he forgot everything but that.

"I didn't know who you were, Becca," he gritted out. "I swear."

"It's all right," she whispered. "I know who *you* are."

And then she arched up on her toes, hooked an arm around his neck, and pressed her mouth to his.

CHAPTER EIGHT

HIS HANDS MOVED to hold her, both of them warm against her shoulders and then tight on her back, but Theo did not otherwise so much as flinch. His mouth was warm, his lips firm beneath hers, and the feel of him, silk and steel, made her shiver uncontrollably.

But Becca forced herself to pull away, though it seemed much more difficult than it should have been, and dropped back down from her toes. He looked down at her, a slight frown between his remarkable eyes, and she had the sense he was trying to figure her out. As if she was the puzzle. She gazed up at him, her lips still tingling from their contact with his. However brief, she could still feel the heat of him, roaring through her veins, making her heart clatter against her ribs.

The paparazzi outside had been terrifying. More like a pack of wild dogs than people, they had pressed in against her, shouting insults and horrible, vicious questions, while flashbulbs went off again and again, blinding her. But safe inside the elevator, she had wanted to forget. Forget…everything. Did it matter that Theo had proved himself to be as ruthless as he'd always told her he was? She knew that should horrify her, but it hadn't. It didn't. After the terrible commotion outside, after the panic that had surged through her and made her wonder if she'd be sucked into the pack of them, whole, Theo had seemed safe in comparison. Or at least, dangerous in an entirely different, somehow more manageable way.

She had felt his hands on her, had seen the heat and the remorse in his penetrating amber gaze, and she just hadn't seen the point of pretending to be anything but just as fascinated by him as he'd accused her of being. And if she had to run the gauntlet of paparazzi, she'd reasoned, if she had to put up with all the downsides of this glittering role she was playing—why not take advantage of the only upside she could see in all of it?

Careful, the practical side of her had cautioned. *You're too emotional right now, this is much too intense....*

But she'd kissed him anyway. She shouldn't have done it, she knew. She might very well live to regret it with her whole heart—and yet she could not seem to feel as badly about that as she knew she should.

Instead, she felt exhilarated, as if she could take a running start from one of Theo's balconies and soar away, high over the proud skyscrapers of Manhattan and into the sky beyond. And yet her eyes still felt too full, too heavy, as if she might cry at any moment. Her hands twitched with the urge to press against her own lips.

It was as if she no longer had control of her own body.

You are entirely too emotional, that prim voice inside of her lectured sternly. *You are letting this crazy situation tie you into knots.*

"I'm sorry," she whispered, because she didn't know what else to say. She felt as if she'd run for miles, and could now only shake slightly, ache too deeply and dream of moving that fast, that far, all over again.

"For what?" he asked quietly, his eyes intent on hers,

burning into her, branding her. "For kissing me? Or for stopping?"

Becca had no idea how to answer that. She felt her lips part, but no sound came out, and a darker fire bloomed into life in Theo's gaze. She could feel it sear into her skin.

But the elevator doors slid open, and Becca tore her gaze away from his. She walked quickly, blindly, into the vast penthouse, only stopping when she realized that she had not caught her breath in some time. That was why she felt very nearly dizzy, she told herself. That was why her skin no longer seemed to fit her correctly.

"And now you run away," Theo said softly, far too close behind her. "Perhaps you are sorry for all of it, after all."

Becca turned, slowly. She had the odd feeling as she did so that the world was altering, right then and there, in that moment. That she would look back on this very second and know, somehow, that after it she had no longer been the same person. That Theo would wreck the Becca Whitney she knew, forever after. And still she turned, unable to stop herself or stave off the inevitable, and he was even closer than she'd imagined. His gaze was still hot and intent, turning her into jelly. Making her want to simply fling herself into his arms, right here in this great room that should have made her feel insignificant. But it didn't. Not today. Not when this man with his tortured gaze looked at her like this, as if he wanted to burn them both alive with the electricity that hummed between them. As if that would be some kind of sacrament.

"Or perhaps that was not you kissing me at all," he said, his voice a low rumble that seemed to move inside of her, as if he was already deep within her. "Perhaps it was one more ghost, conjured into life by that rabble outside."

"Don't!" she gasped at him, hardly able to speak, hardly able to get the word out. But once it was there, between them, and he looked at her so expectantly, she found she could not seem to continue. There was too much noise in her head. Too many cautionary whispers on the one side, and too many treacherously seductive murmurs on the other. As if she really was two people in the same skin, both desperate for control—and neither winning it.

There were so many things she wanted to say. She wanted to explain to him how much it hurt her, though she told herself it shouldn't, that she still didn't know if he looked at her that way for herself, or if he saw Larissa. She wanted to tell him that it didn't matter anyway, because clearly this connection between them was better, hotter, *more* than he could ever have had with another woman, no matter who she was.

But the last thing in the world she wanted to do right now was utter that name out loud. Not when he was so close, so sensually intent, and she could reach out her hand and feel the heat of him. Not when she so desperately wanted to prove that she was no ghost. She was real. Just like him.

"What do you want?" she asked, her voice much too low, much too breathy, to be her own. A frankly sensual smile curved in that hard jaw, and arrowed directly into her core.

"I already told you what I want." His brows rose, and his hands moved at his sides, though he did not touch her. She knew, somehow, that that restraint hurt him. "The better question is, what do you want?"

Becca laughed then, surprising herself. It was the

laugh of a dedicated wanton, low and rich, and came from some deep, feminine place inside of her she'd never encountered before. Some place where she was not conflicted about this man at all. A place where she simply wanted him, no matter how much she struggled against it. And so she laughed, sensual and suggestive, and watched his eyes narrow with desire.

"I think I made myself clear," she said.

He reached out then, and wrapped his fingers around the end of her ponytail, tugging on it gently, making her head dip toward him.

"Be more clear." It was a command. Clear and concise. Why should that make her melt all the more?

"*I* was the one who kissed *you*," she reminded him. "But you didn't seem to care very much for the experience."

What if there was a reason for that? Suddenly, her confusion flooded her. What if she was imagining this fire, this breathlessness? What if it had nothing to do with *her* and everything to do with who she looked like? And what did it say about how far she'd fallen that she might not mind as she knew she should—as she clearly *would,* if she had any self-respect left at all?

"I want you to be certain about what you're doing," he said in that ruthless way of his, that purely masculine command ringing out in his voice. Strong. Certain. And soothing her that easily. "You need to be absolutely sure, Becca. Because I won't be satisfied with *halfway.* Or *once.*"

A prickling sort of heat broke out all over her skin, making her clothes feel too tight, her breaths too shallow, as if she might burst. Into flame. Into pieces. She wasn't sure she cared which.

"Typical," she managed to say, despite the heat and

the ache and the riot in her head, deep in her blood and between her legs. "You've barely kissed me and yet you demand that I decide whether or not I want to sleep with you right here and right now? Is this how you negotiate your business affairs, Theo? All or nothing, based on the faintest and least illuminating of examples?"

"Let's see if you find this more illuminating," he said, with the faintest hint of a smile his eyes glinting, and then he bent his head and took her mouth with his.

Theo did not merely *kiss*. Theo…possessed.

His mouth opened over hers, hungry and demanding, and he angled himself closer, his hands spearing into her hair to hold her and guide her as he took his time with her mouth, tasting her, teaching her, making dark, sensual promises with every touch of his tongue, his lips.

And Becca went wild.

Her arms were around him, testing his wide shoulders and anchoring behind his neck. He bent into her, making her arch toward him, finally pressing her swollen breasts against the hard wall of his chest. He angled his mouth for a better, hotter fit, making her groan against him, and then he undid her completely by pulling her hips flush against his.

He was hard and big, and she felt herself melt all around him.

She could not get close enough. She could not break away. She had the frenzied notion that her whole life had been leading right here, to this kiss. To him.

"Theo…" she murmured, and he shifted, lifting her high against his chest. With a touch, he encouraged her to wrap her legs around his lean waist, bringing her hips tight against his. She felt his hardness against her softness, and moved against him, making them both shudder. He dug his fingers into her hair, pulling out the ponytail holder and tossing it carelessly aside. Freed, her hair fell around them, shielding them in the scent of musk and flowers. And again he took her mouth, with such devastating skill, such resolute mastery, that she felt herself shuddering against him. So much want. So much need.

He made her mindless.

"So tell me," he said against her mouth, his male-ness hard and proud against her, making her want to move, to be as wild as she felt, to writhe and scream and find herself in this hot, bright fire. "Have you seen the light?"

"You know I have," she whispered, her voice broken, her lips slightly swollen from his. "It turns out you are a very illuminating man, after all."

Theo only smiled. Hard. Satisfied. Male.

And then he shifted her in his arms, and carried her up the spiral staircase to his bedroom.

Becca barely noticed the details of the room, all mas-culine colors and shades, everything dwarfed beside the sweeping floor-to-ceiling windows that dominated the far wall. She only had the faintest sense of the city beyond them, and then she was on her back in the middle of the wide, platform bed, and Theo was beside her.

Any teasing had fled somewhere on the walk from the floor below, and Becca could feel the silence all around them, making the fire inside of her burn brighter, hotter. Making the way he looked at her, the way his hands traced patterns along her body, feel something very close to sacred.

He pulled her boots from her legs and let them clatter at the side of the bed. He stripped off his coat and the light, cashmere sweater he wore beneath. And then he came over her, resting in the V of her thighs, making her sigh in some mixture of desire and satisfaction.

He did not speak. He kissed her face, moving from her forehead to her jaw, then down along her neck. His hands tested the weight of her breasts through the silky material of her dress, dragging thumbs over her painfully hard nipples until she arched up from the bed against him.

She felt as if she'd been waiting forever to touch him, to trace his long, lean muscles with her palms, her fingers, her mouth. He was hot to the touch, and smooth, his skin against hers making the world seem to spin around them.

Theo sat back, and looked down at her, his face almost harsh with passion. He pulled her to sitting position and with little ceremony, pulled her dress off and over her head. He let out a small sound when she sat before him in nothing but her bra and panties, and then he reached over and took her face in his hands, guiding her mouth to his.

He kissed her again and again, passion and promise, and this time when his mouth moved from hers he found her breasts, tasting one and then the other through the sheer silk and lace, making her head drop back and her eyes drift closed. His hands smoothed down her abdomen, then around to her back, and she hardly noticed when he pulled the bra from her body. But a jolt of fierce pleasure rocked through her when his lips closed over a hard nipple, pulling the hard peak insistently into the hot, wet depths of his mouth. He did the same with the other, inflicting his delicious torture until she was truly mindless in his arms, bucking against him, trying to ride his hardness as he pressed against her.

He laughed slightly, and tilted her up and toward him, so her legs fell on either side of where he knelt on the mattress. Then he let one hand find its way to her softness. He held her for a moment, making her pant with desire and impatience. She could feel the heat of his hand through the scrap of lace—and could not help the way her hips rolled against his palm, demanding that he end this torture.

But instead, he kissed her, taking her mouth with dizzying skill. Again and again he tasted her, and then he slowly, achingly, worked his big hand into her panties, until he could trace her femininity with his clever fingers. One stroke, another, making her sex flood with heat, making her gasp against his mouth, and then he twisted his wrist and drove one finger deep into her. Then another. Then, still kissing her as if he would never stop, he set an easy, devastating pace. His hot hand against the center of her core, his fingers inside of her, and his mouth against hers.

Becca bucked against him, again and again, clutching at his shoulders, and then she burst into a thousand pieces, sobbing his name into his mouth.

When she came back to herself, she was flat on her back on the bed, her panties were gone, and Theo was laying tender kisses along the undercurve of her breast, the slight swell of her belly and the jutting thrust of her hipbone.

She looked down the length of her own body to see his dark head, shockingly black against her own pale skin, his skin shades darker than hers, the contrast seeming to emphasize how much bigger he was, and how strong. He held her hips in his hands and made love to her navel, and then traveled lower, making the fire she'd thought extinguished roar back into life.

She tried to tug at his shoulders, to pull him away from what seemed far too intimate, far too *telling,* somehow—but he refused to budge. He looked up at her, his eyes nearly gold with desire. She could not help the shiver that ran through her then.

"I want you," she whispered, her hands on him, urging him up. "I want you inside me."

"So forward," he chided her, teasingly, as his hands wrapped around her bottom and tilted her hips toward him. "We hardly know each other yet."

"Theo," she began, even as that drumbeat began again in her, that demanding passion, thudding out her want, her need. Her hunger.

"Luckily," he continued, spreading her thighs even wider with his shoulders as he bent between her legs, "I have the perfect remedy."

And then he leaned down, pressed his mouth against her sex, and tasted her, long and slow and deep.

CHAPTER NINE

SHE CLIMAXED AGAIN almost immediately, but Theo couldn't stop. She was irresistible. He felt off balance, intoxicated—lost in her. And he could not get enough of it.

He tasted her, honey and cream, and though his sex was so hard it ached, he could not tear himself away. She moaned out his name, and he liked it. He liked it far too much. He licked into her, making her shudder and moan, and only when her head thrashed back and forth on the bedcover yet again did he roll away to rid himself of his trousers.

She lay before him like a goddess, like a dream. Her breasts were full and perfect, and tasted like a marvel. Her curves intoxicated him, and he could not get enough of her taste, so delicate and female and *Becca*.

She met him when he came back to the bed, rising up to kneel before him, and he gloried in the feel of her nakedness against his, finally, and the softness of her belly like satin, cradling the hardest part of him.

He wanted her so much it actually caused him something akin to pain. But he could not think about that now. The late-afternoon light cast shadows all around them, but she still seemed to shine, bright and true, in the middle of it.

God, how he wanted that light. How he wanted *her*.

He couldn't wait any longer. He lifted her into his chest, rolled his hips and thrust deep into her.

She cried out, and her head fell back. She moved to put her legs around his waist and he eased them both back down onto the bed. Only then did he move, thrusting deep inside of her and then out again, testing his length, marveling at the slick, sweet fit.

She was his. She was finally his.

He felt as if he'd been longing for her forever. As if she had been crafted for his hands alone, made to fit him perfectly, her body and his like a lock and key. He could feel the dead bolt click over inside of him. He welcomed it.

And then passion took over. He set a hard, demanding pace, and she met him, her hips rising to meet his, her hands urging him on, her nails digging into his flesh. He bent his head to hers and put his mouth against the slender column of her neck, grazing it with his teeth, making her sob out his name. He rocked against her, feeling her stiffen and hearing her moan, and when she climaxed for the third time, she screamed.

He called out her name, and followed.

Much later, she stirred against him, and he felt himself harden yet again, his length still buried deep inside her.

Her startled laughter was husky, still laced with the passion they'd just spent, the fires they'd banked. It moved over his body like a caress.

"Not possible," she murmured. "Not even for the great Theo Markou Garcia."

He grinned, and rolled, so she lay sprawled on top of him, her soft breasts pressed into his chest, her ripe curves his to explore. Watching her expression, he pulled back until he was almost clear of her entrance, then slowly thrust back in. Teasing. Tantalizing. Building the fire anew.

She sighed, pleasure making her features that much softer, that much prettier. *Mine,* he thought. *All mine.*

"I told you," he said, thrusting into her slowly, so very slowly, and watching her mercurial eyes darken with that same need. "Once is not nearly enough."

And then he claimed her lush, wanton mouth with his, and lost himself in her.

Again.

The week had passed in a sensual haze, then continued into the next, and when reality intruded once more in the form of the vile Whitney family, Becca was woefully unprepared.

It was almost as if she'd forgotten the reason she was here at all, she reflected as she put the final touches on her evening's outfit. As if she had just magically appeared in this penthouse, in Theo's bed, and everything that had brought her here was blurred and opaque. Or perhaps she'd simply wished for that to be true, she thought, facing the unpleasant truth.

Because it was far easier to simply live for the hours she and Theo spent in bed, wrapped around each other, exploring each other's bodies with a wild passion and a creative flair that made her shiver to think about, even now. Theo was a man who liked to cover all of his bases. He did his research and he was as determined as he was methodical. He was ruthless, focused and as deliciously, sensually demanding in bed as he was when he acted as her personal trainer. All the qualities that made him an overbearing temporary employer made him a phenomenal, masterful lover.

Oh, the things he could do. And did.

"Wake up," he had ordered her that very morning, his dark voice husky as his hands had streaked over her, as he'd slid deep into her, both waking and arousing her with each deep thrust.

She had burst into flame before she'd remembered where—or who—she was, shattering into pieces all around him.

Becca squeezed her eyes shut for a moment, as that insistent ache pulsed in her core, that same familiar longing welling up in her anew. The more she had him, the more she wanted him, with a hunger that nothing ever seemed to satisfy. That was one more thing she didn't dare think about. One more item she filed away and vowed she'd look at…later.

But tonight she had to face her demons. Her so-called relatives. Tonight, the rude reality of her presence here could no longer be avoided.

She took a last, long look in the mirror, and squared her shoulders. She knew she looked as she should. Like Larissa. She wore her hair in classic Larissa-style, the pale blond strands swept high in front and then cascading to brush her shoulders. She'd picked a simple pale gold dress that shimmered when she moved, picking up the light and seeming to reflect it, as if she was bottled sunshine. She'd done her makeup to perfection, and she'd even started wearing the contact lenses that made her eyes glow green, like a cat's. She was as Larissa as she was likely to get.

And still her stomach was clenched tight, like a pretzel. Like an unbreakable knot. She let her hands rest there for a moment, trying to soothe the clenched feeling away.

"We will dine at Whitney House tonight," Theo had

said over breakfast, that implacable command in his voice. He had not looked up from his computer. It had been as if she had not screamed out his name only a scant half hour before, as if he had not left a mark on her collarbone with his teeth when he'd found his release.

It had been as if they were back to the same place they'd been at the start. So long ago, she'd thought, that at first she hadn't understood what was happening. And when she'd finally comprehended it, she was surprised at how much it hurt. How deeply it seemed to cut into her.

"I can't think of anything I would like to do less," she had said, determined not to show him that he'd struck a blow. Determined, for that matter, not to admit it to herself. She'd lounged in her chair, languid and unconcerned, every inch the pampered little princess she'd been pretending to be for weeks.

She hadn't much cared for the way he'd looked at her then, his amber gaze something much too close to condemning. Or was it simply that he'd reverted to the all-business, hyperfocused version of himself, that she hadn't seen in over a week?

"It wasn't a request," he'd said softly, his voice brooking no argument.

And that simply, he'd reminded her. Of her place. Of the situation. He had not come out and *said* it. He hadn't had to *say* anything.

He might as well have dropped her over the side of the penthouse wall, letting her plummet to the Manhattan street so far below. That was how hard Becca had hit the ground.

Wake up, you fool, she'd mocked herself. *Welcome back to reality.*

Because the harsh truth was that he might want her

in his bed. He might groan out her name and murmur words she was afraid to attach too much importance to in the light of day. He might smile at her sometimes as if she was capable of lighting up his world. But most of all, above all things, he wanted her to pretend to be Larissa. Maybe he'd been pretending she was Larissa already, this whole time.

The thought made her sick to her stomach.

But more fool, she, for putting that possibility—that likelihood—out of her mind for even a moment. Much less for all these days and endless nights that blended together and sat on her, in retrospect, like a great weight.

And she was a fool to the end, because even now, she thought as she walked through the soaring rooms of the penthouse, nodding at the driver who waited for her in the foyer—even now she wished he was here instead of meeting her over at the Whitney mansion, wished she could touch him, wished she could feel that inevitable rush and burn that she was beginning to think would always consume her when she saw him. That it was simply the effect Theo had on her.

He had ruined her, she thought with a flash of something too close to despair, and she hadn't even started the hard part of this charade. At this rate, she'd be lucky to leave in pieces.

Much sooner than she was comfortable with, Becca found herself sitting outside the Whitney mansion, staring up at it from within the depths of the low-slung limousine that had whisked her here from the penthouse's underground garage—the garage that Theo had deliberately not used the day he'd had them run the paparazzi gauntlet.

Funny how that memory made desolation yawn open

within her tonight, when she hadn't minded back when it had happened. Quite the opposite—she had understood so completely it had propelled her directly into Theo's bed, and she had hardly come up for air since.

What had happened to her? She'd known better than to let this happen—she'd known it from the moment he'd strode into that room in the Whitney mansion so long ago now. Her whole body had rioted in warning, aware of the threat he presented. He'd made her display herself for him, he'd ordered her around, and none of that seemed to matter. She could not even work up the appropriate level of outrage now, as she considered her own fall from grace. She had lost herself, she knew. Perhaps forever.

It was the way he looked at her. When she knew he saw *only* her, and it stole her breath and filled her heart. She didn't have it in her to withstand that look. She didn't even want to try.

The car came to a stop, snapping her out of her reverie. She climbed out of the car when the driver opened the door, and paused for a moment as she gazed up at the house. It was not an icon of a bygone era by accident. The mansion rose up from Fifth Avenue, a proud ghost of a bygone age, all flamboyant grace and style. Becca eyed the curved bay windows that opened up over the avenue, the balustraded balconies and the dramatic roof that soared high above in a nod to a French château. The house sprawled the length of the block, self-assured and deeply self-satisfied. It looked different at night, more sinister, or perhaps more impressed with itself as the security lights shone up on its elegant facade, each light carefully placed to highlight and dramatize the house's Gothic appeal.

It was impossible not to feel like the doomed ingenue

marching to her certain end, Becca thought as she made her way up the grand stairs. No matter how very far removed from an ingenue she might have been. Or perhaps it was simply an echo of the last time she'd been in this precise spot. She could hardly remember herself back then, and that was what made her pause in her tracks, right there on the threshold. She looked down at herself, at the elegant dress and the high, fanciful shoes. The luxurious, deep red wrap she'd worn to keep off the night air and the jeweled bag she held in one hand.

A far cry from her ripped-up jeans and battered old hooded sweatshirt, she thought. She had a sudden premonition then—a perfect vision of herself in her old boots, wearing her old clothes, but still with Larissa's hair and this new way of carrying herself, headed back up to Boston, all alone. Some strange hybrid of her cousin and herself, but all, still, in this same body. She should have rolled her eyes at the image, or smirked it away as she would have done, once. But instead, she felt something like sadness well up from deep within. And she couldn't allow herself the time or space to figure out why. This was the den of the enemy. This night was going to hurt, one way or another.

There was no time for sadness.

She reached out before she could think better of it and rang the heavy bell.

Anger, she found not ten minutes later, served her far better. It was a weapon. It could be wielded.

She stood in yet another interchangeably elegant room of this offensively spacious palace, holding a glass of perfectly chilled wine from some unspeakably expensive vintage in one hand, and holding on to her temper with everything else she possessed.

"Well," her aunt Helen said with a sniff, breaking the long and far-from-comfortable silence that had lasted since the moment Becca had been ushered into the room. "The likeness is truly astonishing. There's no debating that."

There was no one else in the large, faintly chilly room. Theo and Bradford, Becca imagined grimly, were closeted off somewhere, no doubt comparing their bank balances and ruining lives. That left only the censorious Helen to serve as the welcoming committee. She sat on one of the fussy, stiff and uninviting-looking chairs near the cold stone fireplace, the face that so greatly resembled her mother's—had Caroline been as coddled and as bitter as this woman—screwed into a disapproving frown.

"One couldn't really imagine how it was possible," Helen continued, her voice the precise cadence and pitch to suggest that she was being scrupulously courteous, when in fact, she was not. "After all, when you appeared here last you were in such a wild, unmanageable state."

"I think by that you mean I looked *poor,*" Becca said smoothly, smiling hard enough to draw blood. Her fingers tightened around the stem of her wineglass, so tight she thought she might snap the glass in two. She loosened her grip. Slightly. "Which I understand, to you, is anyone not in possession of their own private jet and selection of secondary residences. The rest of us simply call that *normal.*"

The older woman stared at her, affront written all over her face. She was like all the other women of her particular station, all the other upper-class East Coast women with their lustrous pedigrees and their Seven Sisters degrees, their carefully selected yet never ostentatious jewelry, and their quiet, pervasive aura of superiority. Her clothes were all understated elegance, her hair carefully bobbed and smooth on either side of her narrow, moderately attractive face. Yet her natural expression, Becca had no doubt, was this very glare she was delivering now, from down the length of her patrician nose.

"A pity Theo couldn't have improved your manners," Helen said. Her smile was razor sharp, and utterly fake. "Although perhaps this is as much as someone like you was capable of improving."

Becca felt frozen and furious all at once—a terrible combination. She forced herself to move with all of Larissa's boneless nonchalance toward the only piece of furniture that did not look as if it would like to judge its occupant—a splendid couch, all bright reds and whites. She sank into it, and schooled her features into bland-ness when she met Helen's gaze once more.

"It can be so difficult to train up the peasants," she said, pretending to commiserate, her voice heavy with irony. "They find it so hard to project the kind of snob-bery that comes so naturally to their betters."

"Whatever her faults," Helen said then, raising her brows, and looking as if it was a heroic act to ignore Becca's last words, "Larissa was at least capable of con-ducting herself like a Whitney when it mattered."

Becca shook her head. "I know this must wound you as deeply as it does me," she said, almost as if she pitied this woman. "But I am, in fact, a Whitney. That you turned your back on your only sister, the better to hoard your treasures in this morgue you call a house, only makes you sad. It doesn't make me any less your niece."

She expected Helen to gasp, clutch at her ubiquitous

pearls, perhaps even swoon. But the other woman was no longer the fluttering, gasping creature Becca recalled from their first meeting in this house. Helen surprised her. She actually smiled slightly, with a hint of something like nostalgia, which made her whole face change. Unexpectedly, it made her look…more like Becca's mother than Becca would have thought possible. She had to swallow hard against the rush of emotion that threatened to swamp her.

"You look nothing like your mother," Helen said after a long, strange little moment, maybe two. "She took after our father's side, like the rest of us. But you sound just like her." She blinked. "It's extraordinary."

This time, the quiet that took over was less tense, if no less fraught with the weight of the past. Becca dropped her gaze to her wine, peering at the golden liquid as if it could solve all of her problems, banish all her ghosts. This was, she thought, perhaps as close as she was likely to come to the happy family reunion she'd imagined so feverishly—and secretly—when she was a girl. There would be no clutching of the lost child to her aunt's breast, clearly—but it was something. Something more than had been there before.

It shouldn't have comforted her. It shouldn't have felt like balm to an old wound.

"You truly do look remarkably like Larissa," Helen said after a moment. She shifted in her chair. "Theo did a wonderful job, as he always does."

"He's a talented man," Becca said dryly, and then regretted it when her aunt's gaze caught hers. There was a certain recognition there—a certain knowledge—that set off alarms all over her body.

"Theo is the most driven, most ruthless man I know,"

Helen said. Purposefully. Deliberately. "He allows nothing to distract him from his goal. Nothing."

Becca felt horribly exposed—as caught out as she'd been in the glare of all those paparazzi flashbulbs. How could Helen know what had transpired between them? Was it imprinted on her face somehow? But she knew it couldn't be. She had worked too hard over the past weeks to make sure her face showed only what she wanted it to. In this case, the ghost of a girl who never got upset about anything, not where anyone could see.

"That sounds like an excellent quality to have in the family company's CEO," Becca said briskly. "Congratulations."

"Nor is he the kind of man to settle for substitutions," her aunt continued, in that same arch, superficially polite tone with the bite beneath. Any tenderness that might have connected them, however briefly, was gone as surely as if Becca had imagined it. Perhaps she had. "You've seen how he lives. Theo demands, and receives, the very best. Nothing else will do."

Becca couldn't help the little laugh that came out of her then. Was it amazement? Or just a kind of horror that this woman was articulating all the fears she had refused to put into words herself?

"I'm sorry," she said. She made herself look Helen in the eye, made herself sit there calmly, her face blank. "Are you warning me about something? Is that what this is?"

"You're out of your depth," Helen said in a voice that was arguably meant to be kind, but sounded like nothing more than the worst kind of condescension to Becca's ears. Helen shrugged delicately. "That's not a judgment, merely a statement of fact. It would be easy to misunderstand things, I'd think. Easy to misinterpret."

She took a sip of her wine, her narrowed gaze much too shrewd. "Far too easy to forget oneself."

Becca could have pretended she didn't understand. But even if Helen didn't know the particulars, it was the casual assumptions that made Becca's blood heat, her temper rise. Because *of course* the poor relative, caught up in these high-stakes games, so wide-eyed and naive, would fall for a man like Theo and fail to see that he was using her as a substitute. *Of course* Helen thought she was that stupid. Helen thought anyone who did not come from her world was that stupid, by definition.

The fact that she was right was not something Becca intended to confront. Not now. Not while Helen looked on.

"You're operating under the assumption that I want what you have," Becca bit out. "What Larissa had. I don't." She laughed again, though it was slightly more wild this time, slightly more bitter. "I want nothing to do with this fake, glittering, poisonous little world of yours, I assure you."

"If you say so," Helen said, gliding to her feet, poised and cool. Her gaze was pitying. "But that does not change the facts of things, does it?"

CHAPTER TEN

IT WAS TIME.

Theo sat at the long, formal dining room table and found himself brooding as he watched his perfect creation, his Becca, shine. She embodied Larissa, just as he'd taught her to do. He thought she was more than Larissa—she had more life in her, more sparkle, than her cousin had ever had. But no one would see her and think anything was amiss; they were far more likely, he reflected, to assume that rehabilitation had finally worked its magic on poor, lost Larissa.

Which meant that he had succeeded. He should have been jubilant. This mad plan that should never have worked seemed set to succeed beyond his wildest dreams. He had created his own little ghost, and now it was time to let her do what she'd been made to do. Haunt. Confuse. And win him back the shares that had been meant to be his in the first place.

It was too bad that he felt as if he was the one already haunted.

"I hope you read your contract carefully," Bradford was saying to Becca, his attention on his elegant plate and the perfect duck that graced it. Other than a sweeping head-to-toe glance when she'd walked into the room, Theo didn't think Bradford had looked at her directly.

"No, I prefer to sign intimidating-looking documents without so much as glancing at them," Becca said mildly, lounging against the back of her chair, her narrowed gaze on Bradford. Her duck lay before her, untouched. "I find it's so much more fun to be disappointed and taken by surprise down the road."

Theo should not have found her as entertaining as he did.

Bradford sniffed. "You're making a good show in the tabloids," he said, in quelling tones. "But your flippant attitude hardly does you credit."

"Funny," Becca said with apparent unconcern, though Theo saw the tension she fought to hide, "but I *did* read the contract. I especially read all the parts that outlined what I had to do, and what I would receive in return for that." Her brows rose in that challenging way that sent heat spiraling through Theo, even here, even now. "But at no point did it mention that I had to impress *you* with my attitude."

Bradford very carefully placed his silverware against his plate, and meticulously touched his linen napkin to his lips. The room fell hushed—the only sound was Helen, drinking deep from her wineglass. Becca, of course, his Quixote, only gazed at Bradford expectantly. Finally, Bradford leveled his cold glare across the table at his niece, who must have seemed to him like his own daughter, brought back from the brink.

Or did Theo ascribe to the man qualities and feelings he did not possess? Theo studied his face, but was not surprised to see no hint at all of anything resembling emotion. Bradford was cold and calculating. He had been that way as long as Theo had known him—interested only in expanding his profit margin, his power base, his investment portfolio. He had hardly paid his wife attention when she had still lived with him, and he had never so much as mentioned her name since she'd taken herself off to France. He had never, as far as Theo knew, given his daughter, his only child, the slightest hint of anything approaching fatherly affection. Theo doubted he was capable of such a thing.

And if *he* was any kind of man, Theo knew, he would stop this scene before it played out. Because he did not have to be a mind reader to know that Bradford would be cruel to Becca. He knew it was inevitable. But he also knew that any sign of protection on his part would only make Bradford worse. And the manipulative part of him—which was, perhaps, a far larger part of him than he was comfortable admitting these days—knew that in order to truly act like Larissa, Becca really ought to live through one of the defining experiences of Larissa's life: dealing with her father.

He also knew that Becca was stronger than Larissa had ever been. Tougher. More fierce. Half Quixote, half warrior. She could handle herself.

So he said nothing at all. And hated himself all the more.

"Blood will tell," Bradford said. His lip curled as he looked at Becca. "And there can be no doubt that yours is certainly a stain upon the Whitney name."

Theo wanted to wring his neck. But instead, he did nothing. This was her battle, however little she might have wished to fight it. He merely sat and watched.

"My blood *is* Whitney blood," Becca replied, with that underlying sting in her voice. She smiled. "Or do you lack a basic understanding of genetics?"

"You are the bastard child of my sister, the whore," Bradford said, in his calm, polite, vicious way.

Theo saw Becca stiffen, saw the faint color that

appeared on her cheeks, but she made no other outward sign that those nasty words had hurt her. Just as he knew he gave no hint that he wanted to put his fist through Bradford's pompous face for speaking to her that way. What a great hero he was, he taunted himself with a wealth of derision. What a man he'd become. And was he any different from Bradford, in the end? Did they not want the same things? It made him sick to consider it in those terms.

"And I want to make sure that you don't have any ideas above your station." Bradford's voice droned on, patronizing and dismissive all at once. "The contracts are ironclad. You will receive your money, and then you will disappear. You will never return. You will never ask for more. You cannot approach the media to sell your story years down the line, when you are desperate yet again." He looked almost kindly as he looked at her. Almost the way an uncle should. "You will sink back into the hole you crawled out of, and stay there."

Helen eyed Theo across the table, her gaze uncomfortably shrewd.

"Surely you don't plan to sit idly by while Bradford eviscerates your…protégé," she said in her insinuating way, the perfect arches of her plucked brows high on her elegant forehead.

Theo didn't much care for the way she looked at him then, nor for the malicious gleam in her eyes.

"Becca can take care of herself," he murmured, as if bored, and did not permit himself to look at Becca directly, no matter how much he wanted to.

And Becca, being Becca, did not cower. She did not cry, as Larissa might have, nor scream out her frustrations. Just as he knew she would not. Instead, she reached out and tapped a finger against the stem of her wineglass, looking as unruffled as if she'd just had a spa treatment. Theo had seen hardened businessmen quail before Bradford's brand of cruelty, before his deliberate and pointed disinterest, but not this woman.

Not his Becca.

"Am I missing something?" she asked after a moment. Her voice was calm. Relaxed, even. Quite as if she was, too—though Theo knew her now, and knew better. "Is there some reason that you think I would *want* to come rushing back to this horrible place? To you?" She laughed slightly. "To the bosom of my family, such as it is? You'll understand, I think, that I would rather be fed alive to a pit of snakes."

"That is easy to say now, and harder to remember when your filthy, depressing little life becomes too much to bear," Bradford replied, his voice smooth. And so certain that he knew how Becca would behave once she left here—so certain that she would come back, hands outstretched. Theo rather thought she would sooner cut them off than give Bradford the satisfaction.

"You speak from what position of authority, exactly?" Becca asked. "Your fevered fantasies about what the lives of those you look down on must be like? Because it certainly can't be experience."

How had he lived so long without her? Theo wondered. And how on earth could he do so again, knowing, now, that she existed?

"The Whitney name has always attracted a bad element," Bradford replied. He indicated Becca with a flick of a finger. "Your father, for example."

Becca did not so much as flinch. Theo winced for her, while she only smirked at Bradford and looked something akin to amused.

"Whereas you, my dear uncle, are such a model for

us all," Becca said, strong until the end, though Theo could hear her temper in her voice, the way it made it that much huskier, that much lower.

She cut her eyes to him then, skewering him with that brilliant, unexpected green, nearly emerald with the contact lenses. He preferred the hazel. The hint of forests. Their gazes clashed across the table, igniting memories, catching fire, hers demanding. Condemning, he thought. Because he was not helping her. He was not defending her. He was simply sitting there, watching, doing nothing at all, while Bradford savaged her.

This was who he was. This shadow of a man. Worthy of nothing and no one, no matter how much wealth he accumulated and power he attained.

Yet even thinking that, knowing it, Theo remained silent. He raised his brows at her, encouraging her to carry on, because he knew she could. She was more than capable. She did not even need him. *Fight,* he thought. *Win.* Her eyes darkened as she read his expression, and her mouth flattened into a hard line. But he knew she'd understood him when she swallowed, nodded slightly and turned away

"You," Bradford said quietly, in that deadly way of his that meant he would raze anything in his path, "would have been better off never born at all. You ruined my sister's life."

Helen gasped from her place down the table. Becca stared at him for a moment, only the faintest whitening of her cheeks any sign that she'd heard Bradford at all, that she'd absorbed that deliberate body blow. Theo saw the pain in her gaze, the betrayal, and a certain flash of resignation that hurt him most of all.

His hands became fists beneath the table.

But this was still her battle.

"You understand this is not my opinion," Bradford said, almost softly. "It is a fact."

Becca pushed back from the table and stood, tossing her napkin onto the glossy surface, every inch of her a study in elegance. Theo understood in that moment that she was not only the most beautiful woman he'd ever seen, but the most precious to him. And, further, that he would lose her. That perhaps he already had.

"I always thought my mother was exaggerating," Becca said after a moment, her voice somehow even, her gaze steady on Bradford as if his cold glare did not bother her at all. "But, in fact, you are even more disgusting than she was willing to admit. I used to look at pictures of Larissa in magazines and wonder how anyone who had so much handed to her could do so little with it—could, in fact, fail so spectacularly." Her lips pursed. "But now I can only wonder how she made it as long as she did. She really never did have a chance, did she?"

"You know nothing about my daughter," Bradford said dismissively. "How could you?"

"As a matter of fact," Becca replied, "I imagine I know more about your daughter than anyone in this room. And one thing is absolutely certain—she deserved more than you. Much more."

She turned and started toward the door, and Theo could not decide if he should applaud her strength or mourn the necessity of her having to display it here, against such cruelty.

"This temper tantrum doesn't matter," Bradford called after her. "You still have to complete your assignment here, or the contract is void."

"Why do you care so much?" Becca asked, looking back over her shoulder, her eyes dark. "You think so little of Larissa—that much is clear." And her gaze lasered through the room, condemning them all anew. Perhaps even Theo. "So why does she have so much power?"

"Power!" Bradford laughed. "She has about as much power as you do."

"And yet you are willing to go to these lengths to fix what you think she broke," Becca said derisively. Incisively, Theo thought. "Maybe this was the only way she knew to hit you where it might actually hurt. If she could wake up, I'd congratulate her—she clearly succeeded."

Her mouth twisted, and her gaze swept over all of them: Bradford with his shark's glare directed straight back at her, Helen sitting so straight and silent, and Theo. Who felt things he could not allow himself to feel and still had not protected her from this. Or even from himself.

"Becca," he said, and though her eyes were Larissa-green, he saw her there, her pride and her determination, her scrappy strength, looking back at him. He would know her anywhere, he thought, no matter who she looked like. And she knew him, too. He could see the recognition, no matter how battered, fill her face for the scant instant before she hid it. When she looked back at her relatives, she had hidden herself away again. She was unassailable. Impermeable. Perfectly Becca.

"I'm tempted to walk right out of here and let her win," Becca said softly. Her chin lifted, and she very nearly smiled. "I still might."

And Theo found it was difficult to do anything but admire her, yearn for her and wonder once more how he could survive losing her, as she pivoted back around and walked from the room.

* * *

Becca was so upset that she could hardly see—something that she only noticed when her breath began to slow again and she realized that rather than walk toward the grand front entrance as she'd intended, she'd managed to completely lose herself in the great mansion.

She came to a stop, pressing her palm into her chest as if that could stop the way her heart pounded, and forced herself to take deep breaths. She looked around, taking in the elegant grandfather clock before her, and a collection of intricately painted blue-and-white vases on a series of narrow tables. She'd never been in this particular hallway before. That in itself was hardly surprising. This place was so big she wouldn't have been at all surprised to discover whole other cities shut away inside of it. Whole other lives. None of them hers.

The riot of confusion and betrayal inside of her threatened to take her out at the knees again, and she had to close her eyes for a moment.

The person she was really angry at, she acknowledged, was herself.

What had she expected? She had told herself that she wanted one thing and one thing only: money to help Emily. And she had believed that, too. Theo had been an unforeseen complication, but she'd honestly imagined that she could handle that, handle him. She'd believed that no matter what might have happened, she was still focused on her goal.

Oh, what a liar she was. Even to herself. And she hadn't even known it until tonight. Until now, when it seemed everything lay about her in ruins, though she stood in such august surroundings, and she wondered how broken she was after all. Because suddenly, there was no escape from the truth.

It was sick, she thought now, and sad, and any number

of other things she felt too raw to face, that there had been that part of her that had wondered if maybe, once these vile, cruel people had seen her all dressed up like Larissa—the one, some still-hurt part of her reminded her, they'd loved enough to keep—they might have had second thoughts about Becca. About how they'd treated her all these years. About how easily, how happily, they'd forgotten about her.

The reality of that lay on her like a great, wet blanket, miserable and awful, and hating herself for her own naïveté only made it worse.

She'd thought she was so tough, so prepared for this world and what it could do. She'd thought she was immune. But instead, she was still the little girl who didn't understand why the rest of her family didn't love her. The little girl who believed, damn Bradford, that she truly had ruined her mother's life. It didn't matter how many times she argued that little girl into submission— the truth was in how hollowed out she felt right now, how scraped raw, by the things that awful man had said to her.

And worse, from the grim knowledge that he believed those things to be true. Worst of all—there was a huge part of her that believed it, too.

She was the beggar at the feast and always had been, no matter how many times she told herself she didn't want what they had. That didn't mean she could understand, even now, how easily they could deny her.

She hated that it hurt her. That Bradford had hurt her. That Helen's moment of near tenderness had fooled her, even momentarily, into believing these people could be anything less than monstrous.

And more than that, she hated that Theo had gotten so far under her skin, had come to matter so much, that she had actually believed the way he looked at her. She had actually believed that she could handle Bradford herself, that it would not leave this deep wound. That she could be the person Theo seemed to believe she was. Strong enough to fight that battle without his help. Strong enough not to need him. Strong enough to walk right out of that door as if she was perfectly fine on her own. And for a few moments in that dining room, she'd believed it. She'd believed that Theo was there for her, watching silently, and would have jumped in had she needed it. She'd *believed*.

It made her want to collapse on the floor and cry, right here in this hushed hallway, because she knew better.

She was alone. She had always been alone. She'd been the odd girl out in the little family her mother had made with her husband and Emily; the shameful memory of Caroline's sordid past and reduced circumstances. Then, after Caroline had died, she'd truly been on her own, fighting with all she had to keep Emily with her—and to live up to her mother's wishes, as the very least she owed to the woman who had lost everything for her. So why should the fact that she was alone here, in this alien place where cruelty seemed as much a part of the decor as the recognizably famous paintings on the wall, make her stomach ache, her eyes water? Why should this come as any kind of surprise?

Why, she asked herself as she headed toward the end of the hall without knowing she meant to move, had she thought for even a moment that anything should be different? Light spilled out of a room up ahead of her, and so she made her way toward it—but her mind was far, far away.

She thought of Theo's dark head, bent to hers. She

thought of his hot mouth, his demanding hands. Her body sang out for him as if he was beside her, and she had to bite back something she feared was much too close to a sob. She would have slapped herself if she could have, because she knew, suddenly, what she'd been denying for much too long already. She knew why she'd so foolishly expected anything at all from a man she should have viewed as nothing but her enemy.

She loved him. A bitter sort of laugh escaped her lips then, echoing down the hall. How could this have happened? How had she let it? But there it was. The truth of it moved in her like a song, high and sweet and sure, but it was not one she was likely to let herself sing.

She was an idiot. A fool of the highest degree. But there was no getting around the facts of it. The truth. She was not the sort of person who fell into bed with just anyone, no matter how beautiful they might be, or how unusually compelling she might find them. She'd known on some level when she'd turned to him for comfort after the paparazzi gauntlet that he'd put her through deliberately. She'd known even sooner, when she'd been so desperate to understand how he could possibly feel as he did for the shallow, seemingly spiteful Larissa. And she'd certainly known this past week or so, when she'd managed to put her reason for being here, and Emily herself, out of her mind, all to lose herself in him.

"Congratulations, Becca," she told herself, her voice little more than a whisper, hushed by the wealth and finery surrounding her, her high heels sinking into the plush Oriental rug that stretched toward the light. "You've managed to make a bad situation that much worse."

She loved him, she thought. She loved Theo Markou Garcia, a man who loved money and power above all things. A man who thought he was in love with a woman he'd hardly known—a fantasy, a dream. A man who would never, could never, love her back. Not even if he wanted to, and she very much doubted he did. After all, as Helen had said, he was a man who wanted the very best. Not its stand-in. Not its low-rent stunt double.

She reached the end of the hallway, and stepped into the room that waited there, brightly lit and notably different from the rest of the house. The door was wide-open, so she moved into what looked like a sitting area, all clean lines and a brisk, contemporary sensibility. She drifted toward the windows, vaguely imagining that she'd be able to figure out where she was in the house if she could see the street, and only when she was halfway there did she catch something out of the corner of her eye.

There was another room, leading off this one. Becca stopped, as her heart seemed to drop to her stomach with the force of a blow. She sucked in a breath and turned, not believing what she could see right there, right in front of her.

The adjoining room was cool and blue and dominated by the hospital bed in its center. There were machines and IV trees clustered around it, but Becca didn't notice them. She hadn't even heard the gentle beeping until now, when she was much too close. She saw only the slight figure on the bed, unmoving beneath the blankets, her pale hair spread out around her like a halo. So fragile. So small. So incapable, it would seem, of causing the commotion she had—both in this world of hers and, Becca thought in no little shame, inside of her.

Larissa.

CHAPTER ELEVEN

MINUTES COULD HAVE passed, or hours, and still Becca stood there in the doorway, watching the woman she looked like—yet who was still a stranger to her—fade away into nothing on that bed.

Not that Larissa was fading, necessarily. Becca wasn't a doctor. What she knew about comas came largely—and presumably inaccurately—from the soap operas she'd watched when home from school as a child. But it seemed impossible to reconcile the person she knew—the Larissa of the diaries she'd read, the photographs she'd studied, the vast and varied tabloid appearances she knew so well—with this wan creature, so silent and still.

It felt as if the ground shook beneath her feet, though she knew on a more rational level that nothing moved. Nothing external. Becca shot out a hand and held on to the doorjamb, unable to fully take in what she was seeing—much less the howling emotional reaction that charged through her like a tidal wave.

We are the same, she thought, and she shook her head slightly to clear it, because thinking such a thing made her feel dazed. There was a faint ringing in her ears then, and her heart seemed to thud hard against her chest.

She had had so many opinions about Larissa over the years, opinions that had solidified over the past weeks. She had been so sure she knew her, that she *understood* her, and that Larissa had been nothing more than a spoiled, arrogant little princess. She'd thrown those words at Bradford, but she hadn't truly meant them. How could she have? She hadn't, even then, *understood*.

But for some reason, she thought she did now.

It had something to do with how frail Larissa seemed. It made Becca see her as…someone else, someone hurt and helpless, someone who was more or less the same age that she was and did not deserve this kind of end. Or any of the rest of this madness. It seemed to erase all those tabloid pictures from her head, made her reassess all the conclusions she'd reached about her cousin's character in these weeks of poring over her every move. It made Becca realize that Larissa was…not so different from Becca, when all was said and done.

It felt very nearly revolutionary to think such a thing.

But they were the same. Chess pieces, as expendable as pawns. Staring at the cousin who looked so much like her, enough that she could pass for her, Becca had a flash of unpleasant and searing insight. *They were the same.* They were both of them formed by the monolith of the Whitney fortune, the Whitney legacy, the Whitney name. Larissa by being thrown headfirst into all of it since birth, Becca by being denied access to it by virtue of her illegitimacy.

Had either one of them ever had a chance?

Who might they each have been—if they hadn't been Whitneys?

"Becca."

Her eyes slipped closed at the sound of his voice, but

not because she did not want to hear it. She suspected that no matter what, no matter where, her whole being would leap with joy at the sound of Theo's dark tones. Even now. Even here.

Even knowing the futility of her own feelings.

"You should not be in here," he said, as his hand came down on her shoulder, his thumb gently smoothing over her bare skin, soothing her that easily, despite everything.

"It's not as if she can complain, can she?" Becca asked, but she turned away from the bed and looked at him.

She didn't know what she expected to see. She felt as if she'd lived through a wholescale sea change, an earthquake of sorts, and surely such a thing should show on her face, shouldn't it? Surely it should alter everything she came into contact with—but Theo was as he always was. Elemental. Electric. His dark, brooding eyes connected with hers, seeing far too deeply into her, and she felt that same, inevitable fire kindle anew inside of her, making her thighs clench, her nipples tighten into high, hard points.

Loving this man was perhaps the most profoundly stupid thing she'd ever done. She knew this with a deep, abiding certainty. But looking at him, taking in his enigmatic expression and his breathtaking masculine beauty, shown to such advantage in the exquisite suit he wore so easily, she could not see how she could have done anything differently. How she could have saved herself.

"What is it?" he asked softly, reaching out and tracing the line of her cheek with his fingers.

"Nothing I have any intention of discussing," she said, truthfully enough. It was astonishing how hard it was not to simply blurt out her feelings. And how, though she knew better, some desperate part of her wanted to cling to the possibility that he was the man she imagined him to be—the man who, she sometimes thought as he moved within her and she held him so close to her, felt more for her than perhaps even he knew.

But she was not that colossal a fool.

Not yet.

"You handled Bradford well," he said after a moment, his dark eyes searching hers.

"I assumed that was the point of the exercise." She smiled wryly. "Was it not?" She had never felt more vulnerable, and yet this practiced veneer had snapped into place, keeping her safe even when she knew she was not.

"I wish I knew," he muttered, but his voice was so low, only the barest thread of sound, Becca wondered if she'd imagined it. Just as she wondered at the flash of something far darker she saw move through his eyes— something she might have called regret.

But this was one of the most powerful men in the world. This was not a man who felt regret—for anything. And certainly not for her.

"Come," he said after a strained moment, heavy with portents and signs she could not begin to decipher. "Let's go home."

He held out his hand, and she took it. She did not question her own eagerness, her own acquiescence. Her time was limited here, she knew, and she was not about to pretend, simply out of spite, she did not want him in any way she could get him. What would be the point? She was the one who would suffer.

And she had the very real fear that there would be suffering enough, when all of this was done.

She did not look back at Larissa as he led her away.

She did not need to. She knew somehow that Larissa would be with her, the true ghost, ever after.

He woke before dawn. The room was gray and Becca was not in his bed where she belonged.

He jackknifed up, and the panic that had seized him eased when he saw her, wrapped in the coverlet and curled up on the leather chaise that looked out over his private balcony, and his own stunning view of Manhattan, shining in the early-morning gloom.

Yet his view right now put all of that to shame.

He rose from the bed, unconcerned with his own nakedness, and moved across the room. At some point she heard him, and swiveled around, her mouth curving in welcome. But not before he'd seen the desolation written so plainly across her face, that she worked to conceal as she turned.

He wanted to demand that she tell him what bothered her, so he could fix it at once—but he did not dare. There was the all too real possibility that what had chased her from his bed in the middle of the night was him. Or any one of the many parts of this situation that would not—could not—change.

So he did not speak. Instead, he reached down and picked her up, holding her against him as he sat down in the chaise himself. He deposited her between his legs, settling her against him, her elegant back snug against his chest. He could smell the subtle fragrance of her hair, and wrapped his arms around her as if he could hold the world away from the both of them. As if he could keep everything else out.

She sighed, her breath fanning across his arm, making his skin heat, making him hard and ready. He always wanted her. He could no longer remember what it was like to want anything or anyone else.

"Emily was so smart, even as a little girl," Becca said after a moment or two, her voice hushed in the early-morning quiet. "It's always been clear that she was destined for better things than the rest of us."

Theo did not speak. He smoothed his hand through her hair, admiring the satiny texture, the enchanting hint of flowers that teased his senses.

"My mother used to call her our little professor," Becca said, and laughed. She shifted in his arms. "Mom wasn't anything like *them*," she said in a low voice. "She might not have made the best choices when it came to men, but she wasn't like them at all. She was kind. Funny. I always remember her laughing, no matter how bad things were." She dragged in a ragged-sounding breath. "She was never cruel."

Theo did not have to ask who *they* were.

"Bradford and Helen have calcified in their own sense of consequence," he said. "It's a side effect of that kind of wealth."

"Excessive?" she asked dryly.

"Hereditary," he said, smiling against the back of her glossy head. "They did nothing to earn the fortune they so enjoy, so they are overzealous in their need to protect it at all costs. They care about nothing else. Not their spouses. Not their children. Not their own sister."

He felt her shiver, and then she was turning in his arms, swiveling around until she faced him. He helped her, holding her as she settled with one leg on either side of his, kneeling up over him, only the coverlet separating them.

For a long, timeless moment, she only gazed down at him. Her eyes were big, her expression solemn, and

Theo could do nothing but meet it. And hold her, even as the coverlet slid down her shoulder, exposing the swell of her breast, just inches from his mouth.

"I want you," she whispered, and her voice was too heavy, her gaze too troubled—but then she leaned down and kissed him, and he let it go. Because her mouth tasted sweet and warm, and he couldn't get enough of it. Of her.

And because he did not want to start digging into the things they kept hidden from each other here. He was too afraid of what they might find.

She controlled the kiss, angling her head for a better fit, and he let her. He let her tease him. He let her play. And each time she deepened the kiss, he let himself taste her as he wanted to do, hot and wet and *his*.

Her breath quickened, and she moaned slightly against his mouth. He reached between them and pulled the coverlet aside, pulling her close to him when she was finally, gloriously naked. Her skin soft and hot against his. Her breasts, tipped in pink and taut against his tongue. And the softest part of her, melting against him, driving him insane.

"If you want me," he whispered, his voice thick with desire, "then take me."

And she did.

Becca took him deep inside of her, shivering in mindless ecstasy as she felt the hot, hard length of him filling her, making her want to cry out loud.

She didn't understand what had happened here, in the not-quite-dark, but she could feel the dampness on her cheeks, and she could see the tortured look in his gaze, and she rode him. She simply moved her hips in an ancient, feminine motion, and destroyed them both.

He called out her name. She heard herself sigh. He pressed his mouth to her neck, then traveled all along her collarbone, his breath hot and his mouth too delicious to bear. And still she rode him, abandoned and powerful, slick and hot, rocking them both closer and closer to the edge.

His hands stroked her back, traced patterns against her skin. He held on to her hips, and set his own pace for a while, making her whole body arch backward, offering herself up to this pleasure. To his touch. To him.

Her first climax hit her, fast and wild, and it was not until the keening noise faded away that she realized she'd cried out in the first place. Theo laughed against her neck, a sensual, stirring sound. He pulled her closer to him, his hips moving fast now, thrusting harder and harder, giving her no chance to recover.

Aftershocks still raced through her, but she met his thrusts, clenching her hands against his shoulders, her gaze heavy-lidded as she looked down at him. His face was severe in his own passion, his mouth set, his eyes glittering. And inside of her, he was so big, so hard. *Hers*. Here, now—hers.

And still he moved. He bent and took a nipple into his mouth, as her hips moved even more urgently in time with his. The searing jolt of pleasure lit her up, from her taut nipple down into her core, and when he pressed his fingers against her sex, she shattered yet again.

This time, he followed. This time, Becca sagged against him, and when he shifted her so she lay curled up against his chest, she could only smile sleepily, and then doze. Content. And more deeply in love than she dared admit, even to herself. Even then.

When she woke again, the sun was blazing in through the windows, and Theo was seated at the foot of the chaise, fully dressed in his slick, off-putting corporate finery, watching her.

The smile that came so automatically when she saw him faded as she took in the grimness of his expression, the set of his jaw. She sat up, pushing her hair away from her face, and pulling the discarded coverlet over her, suddenly chilled. She felt herself flush, deep and red, and wondered with no little despair how he could still reduce her to that, after everything they'd done. After last night.

She only gazed at him, refusing to ask, and eventually he straightened his shoulders, his dark eyes never leaving hers.

"The time has come," he said, expressionless. But she no longer believed the mask he wore. She eyed him, seeing the temper and the anguish hidden in that demanding dark gaze. "Chip Van Housen's birthday party. It's an elaborate affair, but presents the perfect opportunity for you to lure him back to his apartment and find that will."

"Chip Van Housen," she echoed, as if testing out the name. "Hasn't he wondered why his lover has failed to reach out to him this whole time? Surely he would be able to find her no matter how private her facility is supposed to be?"

"He wonders loudly and profanely," Theo said matter-of-factly. "Often several times a day. He is more than happy to believe my jealous rage is what keeps her from contacting him."

"Fine," she said. She cleared her throat, wondering why he was still looking at her like that, as if she'd already failed him. *As if you're already lost to him,* some voice suggested. *As if you always were.* She ignored it. "Are you opposed to birthday parties?" she asked mildly, though it cost her to sound so nonchalant. "Is that why you're sitting there like a—"

"Tonight, Becca." His voice was hard, and she told herself that was why it seemed as if everything around them shattered, as if they were only fragments themselves, all of it broken into a thousand pieces. And yet they still sat here, so politely. So quietly. Staring at each other while the world ended. He cleared his throat. "The party is tonight. You can be home in Boston in a matter of days."

And that was that. That was the end, right there. And he'd said it so unemotionally, as if all that had ever mattered to him was this deception she would perform, and all the rest had simply been filling time. Waiting.

Just as Helen had warned her. Just as she'd suspected herself, in her more lucid moments. Just as he'd promised from the start, by promising nothing at all.

It took everything she had to pull in a breath, to meet his gaze evenly, to conjure up some hint of a smile.

It didn't matter that her heart felt broken in her chest, jagged and dangerous, likely to puncture her lung and kill her where she sat. It didn't matter. Because she had signed a contract, and everything else had been a daydream, and she knew her place. She always had, hadn't she?

So she smiled, damn him, with everything she had.

"Tonight," she echoed, fighting to keep the dullness from her voice, the ache from her eyes. "At last."

And if she wanted to break down, curl into a ball and cry, she kept that to herself.

CHAPTER TWELVE

BECCA HAD NEVER LOOKED more beautiful than she did tonight, Theo thought as a kind of bitterness and a pounding, clawing feeling he suspected must be jealousy, real jealousy—though he had never felt such a thing before—surged through him. Theo lounged in the armchair in her dressing room, eyeing her as she put the finishing touches on her outfit. It was not that she looked so much like Larissa—though she did. It was that she was so clearly, adamantly *not* Larissa to his eyes. He could see her strength, her courage. Her intelligence and wit. It lit her up from within in a way Larissa never could have matched.

He wanted her in ways he had never wanted Larissa. In ways he had never imagined before he met her.

He did not want her to do this. Every cell in his body protested the very idea—though he was well aware he was the one who had asked her to do it. Who *needed* her to do it.

He could not understand himself.

Her final outfit was vintage Larissa, yet with a fresh twist. The dress was bold, seeming to bare all while cleverly managing to show very little. It alternately clung and draped, making her seem ethereal. Untouchable. She'd gone for a smoky look around her eyes, and had left her hair wild around her shoulders. Her long, perfectly toned legs went on for several lifetimes before they ended up in scandalously impractical shoes.

She looked edible, and he wanted a taste. A feast.

How was he possibly going to hand her over to a lowlife like Van Housen? Even if it was only for a little while, and for a specific purpose? *She was his.* He had never been more sure of anything. And it still didn't matter.

Because he had to have those shares. He had to have the control he'd never had as a child. He had never given up, not at any point along the way. He couldn't start now. He didn't know how.

But what he could not seem to understand was why that should seem to him, tonight, like a deep character flaw instead of his greatest strength.

"Tell me again," she said in a low voice, inspecting her mascara in the mirror. "I can't wrap my head around how, exactly, you think I'll be able to fool this man into thinking I'm a woman he knows. Biblically."

"You understand how," Theo said, mildly enough. "You simply don't want to believe what I've already told you, several times."

"Because it's absurd," she said. She took one last, hard look at her reflection, then pivoted to look at him. "He'll know something's wrong. *Off.*"

"Possibly." Theo shrugged. "But you are underestimating the power of suggestion, Becca. When you arrive, everyone, including Van Housen, will assume you are exactly who you appear to be. No one will look at you and think, that's not *quite* Larissa—I wonder if it could be her cousin instead, made up to look like her?"

"You really believe that I can simply walk up to this

man and convince him that I'm someone he's known his entire life?" Her voice was skeptical. And the look in her eyes made him feel restless. Guilty. "And that he won't suspect a thing?"

"That has been the point of this entire exercise, has it not?" His voice was colder than he meant it to be. Harsher. Her lips pressed together, and something dark moved through her bright emerald eyes.

"Indeed, it has." She smiled, though it seemed brittle.

"You could be her twin," he said, and there was a great pressure in him suddenly, some terrible danger lurking near that he could sense but could not avoid. He could do nothing but look at her, losing her with more and more certainty, with every word he spoke. "I could mistake you for her myself."

He saw how stricken she looked for one single split second—before she hid it away, her smooth, tough exterior slamming back into place.

He hated himself. He wanted to hold her. He wanted to stop all of this right here, right now, when the only people they'd hurt were themselves. While there was still time.

But he was not a man who knew how to lose. How to walk away. How to do anything but win, by any means necessary. Even this.

Even if winning this long battle for Whitney Media meant losing Becca. He did not know how he would live without either—and he'd wanted that damned company first.

"All right, then," she said, dropping her gaze as if what she'd seen in his was too much, too upsetting. "We might as well get going, then."

* * *

The ride over to Van Housen's exclusive party, thrown in what was sure to be a deliberately intimidating club in the West Village, was excruciating.

Becca felt hot, then cold. Feverish. She could not do this. She could not.

And yet she had no choice. Not simply because she'd signed that damned contract, but because she knew how terribly Theo wanted those shares. How he even believed he needed them, as if they would complete him—make up, somehow, for his childhood. And if she had it in her power to give them to him, how could she do anything but?

No matter what it cost her. No matter what it took.

But, God, how could she *do* this?

"You must make sure he takes you back to his apartment following the party," Theo said as the car slowed in a sea of yellow taxicabs, all fighting their way up the avenue.

"I know," she said, not looking at him. She sat there, tense and rigid, and tried to tell herself that everything would be okay despite all clear evidence to the contrary. That all of this would work out somehow—but she couldn't quite believe it.

"Do you?" He turned then, trapping her, and she was thrown back to the day she'd first met him, when he'd looked at her just like this—so calculating, so cold. She wanted to squirm away from him, put distance between them, because she feared that what she truly wanted to do was throw herself into his arms and make him put a stop to this cold and nasty little nightmare.

But it was no nightmare—it was the situation Theo had created. Deliberately. This night had always been coming. This was always how this would all end. How had she let herself forget it?

"Of course," she hissed, temper mixing with hopelessness and making her sound far braver than she felt. "I may have agreed to play dress up and prostitute myself on your orders, Theo, but that lapse in judgment does not affect my ability to understand what's expected of me."

His amber eyes gleamed, boring into her, but she couldn't bring herself to look away, to give even that much. Suddenly it seemed as if everything—the whole world, her heart, this terrible night—hinged on her ability to hold her own. To challenge him. To...not meekly accept tonight what she'd signed up for in such ignorance weeks before.

"I do not recall asking you to prostitute yourself," he bit out. She tilted her head slightly to one side, considering him for a moment.

"What do you think will happen?" she asked lightly, though she could feel her own temper, her own fear, beneath. "When this man sees his lover walk into the room, after all these weeks, what do you think he will expect of her when he takes her home? A cozy chat?" She laughed, though it was a hollow sound. "That's not very realistic, is it?"

"Let me make sure I fully comprehend you," he said, seemingly from between his teeth. "Your expectation is that you will have to sleep with Van Housen to get the will?"

She shrugged with far more nonchalance than she felt, refusing to look away from him, no matter how grim his amber-colored gaze grew.

"How else could this play out?" she asked. "This is real life, Theo, not some game. Real people will presumably have real expectations. Are you pretending you haven't considered the possibility?"

She should not have latched on to that flash of temper that he reined in so quickly, nor clung so tightly to the look of something very like anguish that shone briefly in his eyes. The truth was, this was Theo. He might very well feel any number of things. But he wanted that will more. He wanted those shares. She even understood why—he was a man who came from nothing, and had built this whole life for himself with nothing but his determination, his single-minded focus. What was she next to all of that? At best, she was one more sacrifice he'd have to make in service of his ambitions, no doubt one among a great many.

If her heart was broken, that was no one's fault but her own.

"Van Housen is usually entirely too addled by whatever substance he happens to be using to threaten anyone's virtue," Theo said quietly. "The only thing I would worry about, if I were you, is the possibility of his getting sick. Perhaps all over you."

"Please." She leaned back against the seat, and scoffed at him. "He will be reuniting with his longtime lover, and you think he'll simply swoon out of the way? How convenient your imagination is, Theo. But I think you'll find real life is rarely so neat and orderly."

A muscle moved in his jaw, and he reached over to pull a strand of her hair between his fingers, tugging on it gently. Why should so simple a gesture make her ache inside, make her hover too close to tears?

"You seem unduly eager to live up to your worst expectations of this evening," he said, his voice a ribbon of sound, a low growl.

"I'm *realistic*," she contradicted him. She met his gaze, challenge and plea. "Wasn't this what you wanted,

Theo? Isn't this what all of this has been about? Creating the perfect honey trap?"

"No!" he gritted out, and she could see it cost him. She could see how he fought himself. She should not take a kind of pleasure in that. She should not let hope cling so hard to her heart, making it swell when it should know better. When *she* should know better.

"Then what?" She was taunting him, goading him. She couldn't seem to help herself. He moved closer now, his hands taking her shoulders in a tight grip, hauling her to him, his hard mouth a scant, tortured breath from hers.

"I don't want him touching you," he whispered, so low she almost didn't hear him at all, and then he kissed her.

He claimed her. Possessed her utterly. His mouth took and took, branding her. And she exulted in it, feeling fire surge into a wild blaze beneath his hands, wriggling closer to him on the seat, her whole being focused on this kiss, on his mouth, on *Theo*....

But then he set her away from him, his face shuttered. Blank. He sat back and stared out the window, his expression brooding. Distant. And she knew. Before he opened his mouth, she knew.

"I must have that will," he said, his voice hoarse. As if it hurt him, too.

"Of course you must," she replied, not at all successful at keeping the bitterness from her voice, even as her lips still tasted of his kiss, even as her whole mouth felt deliciously swollen, even as she fought to keep herself from pulling him close and losing herself in him one more time.

"You say that as if I have deceived you in some way," he said, still looking out at the city streets, the lights of the bodegas and the ebb and flow of people and cars, the famous pulse of Manhattan just outside the window. "As if this was not the plan from the start. The plan to which you agreed, and for which you will be handsomely compensated."

She laughed then, because of course he was right, and hadn't she been telling herself the very same thing? But hearing him say it cracked something inside of her, ripped it right open, and she couldn't seem to help the feelings that swamped her then. Anger. Betrayal. Deep, deep hurt. The love for him that made her want to fix this, fix him, *fix it* somehow.

And beyond all that, her fatalistic understanding that, as usual, she would not be the one chosen here. She was the discarded child, the Whitney family bastard. Never the golden girl. Never the first choice—always the substitute. She would not win him. She would win nothing. She would leave with her motherís estate, Emily's tuition money, a new hairstyle, memories that she would hoard for a lifetime, and the weary knowledge that she was a survivor. So she would survive this—him—too, little as she could imagine it now. She would. That was what she always did, didn't she? One way or another.

It all added up to more than she'd had when she'd come here, she thought, and wanted nothing more than to give in to the heat that threatened to spill from her eyes. But she couldn't. She just couldn't, not even here, when the wretched little truth of her feelings for him—and more to the point, the paleness of his for her—was so horribly, spectacularly clear to her.

None of it made her want to spare *his* feelings. Not when hers were in shreds all around her.

"You decided what kind of man you wanted to be long before you met me, Theo," she said then, sadly. His head snapped around, and she found her knee jumping again in agitation. She pressed it down with both hands, amazed to see that her fingers weren't shaking.

"I beg your pardon?" His voice was icy. Or was that pain? How terrible that she wanted it to be. She *wanted* to hurt him, she acknowledged, because she wanted to know if it was possible for him to *be* hurt, especially by her. Because—she could admit—some part of her clung to the idea that it would mean something if he felt what she felt, or even some small part of it. It had to. Didn't it have to?

"This is who you are," she said, because she had nothing to lose. She had nothing at all. So why not speak the truth, at the very least? "This will is more important to you than anything else."

"You don't—" he began, his eyes so very grim, but she couldn't seem to help herself.

"More important than me, to be sure," she said, interrupting him.

"Becca…"

"Don't!" she blurted out, that great well of despair crashing over her, threatening to drown her then and there. Somehow, she kept her head above the water. Somehow. "Don't pretend that this is something that's not."

"Maybe it is," he said, stealing her breath, but he was shaking his head, his eyes so intent on hers. It seemed as if centuries stretched between them, as if they hung suspended in time, and she hardly noticed when the car slid to a stop at the curb.

He reached over and took her hand, holding it in his, and she wanted to howl—to scream—to rage. To weep. But she only sat there, captured by him as securely as if he held her in his fist, and wanted what she couldn't have. Again.

"But it doesn't change a thing," he said, sealing their doom. "It can't."

Becca had no memory of exiting the car, but she was on the sidewalk too quickly, shivering slightly. She told herself it was the cool night air, the wind that picked up when it slid through the urban canyons and teased at her skimpy dress. But she wasn't fooling anyone, least of all herself.

"Becca," Theo said, her name a command. And, as ever, she found herself heeding it—hating that she stopped walking. Hating that her body responded to him no matter what her head demanded. She despaired of herself.

"We can have nothing else to talk about," she gritted out at him as he drew close. Part of her wanted to shake off the hand he put on her arm—but only a part. The rest of her wanted to purr like a cat, to bask in the heat of him, the strength. "I am all too aware of who Van Housen is and how I'm to approach him. I am apparently more cognizant of the potential dangers of the evening than you, but as I am the one who will suffer through it, I suppose that makes sense."

"I don't want you to do this," he said in a gravelly voice, as if it was torn from him, as if he hardly knew what he would say before it was out there.

Hope warred with fatalism, and she only stared at him. Wishing. Hoping. Yet not believing this could end any other way but the way they'd planned. How could it?

"Then tell me not to do it." She was whispering, but at least she was not begging. At least she was keeping her tears at bay. And the pleading she could feel swirling around inside of her, so close to spilling out. At least she still had her pride—and she had the sickening feeling that it might be the only thing she'd leave here with.

"Becca..." he said again, his thumb stroking the bare skin of her arm, his body so big, so dangerously lean and powerful, blocking out the whole of Manhattan. "I wish I could change all of this."

"You can." She shook her head, more to fend off the coming tears than anything else. "You are the only one who can."

His head dipped down, and he looked defeated. This strong, capable man. This man who had climbed to such unimaginable heights, all on the strength of his will. His desire. His ferocious and unwavering focus. Her heart seemed to stutter in her chest, and she let her fingers drift up to his lean jaw, holding him.

It was one thing to poke at him. But she could not bear to see him truly hurt, no matter what she'd thought.

For a moment they stood there, holding each other so gently, as if they were not on a city street at all—as if they could stand there forever, taking strength from each other's touch, aching as one.

"I wish I could be a better man," he said finally, quietly, his eyes tortured when they met hers. "But I don't know how."

Becca wavered slightly in her high, impossible shoes, and had to bite her lip to keep from sobbing outright. She had known this would hurt. She'd known it for what seemed like forever. But she hadn't expected that it would hurt him, too. Or that it would hurt her quite this much. She couldn't seem to breathe.

She stepped back from him, though everything in her screamed in protest. His hand dropped away, and he was blurry through the unshed tears, and then she turned and started walking toward the club entrance.

She blinked back the tears, squared her shoulders and told herself to breathe.

She would do this. She would. Somehow, she would.

When he called her name again, she stiffened, but did not turn around. The velvet ropes and red carpets were only steps ahead of her, and she honestly didn't know how much more of this she could live through. It had already left scars so deep they were better called wounds, and she doubted she would ever heal.

And she couldn't take much more of it. She simply couldn't.

"Becca," he said again, and he was closer, too, and so this time she whipped around, her nerves fraying almost to the breaking point.

"No more!" she snapped at him, poking a finger toward his hard chest. "This is going to be hard enough without you making it a hundred times more difficult! You have to either let me go inside and handle this myself, or—"

"No," Theo said. "Don't go inside."

But he did not look happy about that. He didn't even look tortured, or grimly determined—or any kind of thing that might make sense. If anything, he looked dazed, and she followed his gaze to the phone he held in his hand.

"What is it?" she asked. "What's happened?"

He rubbed his hand over his face, and then, at last, his amber gaze connected with hers—but he was miles away. As unreachable as he'd been way back at the beginning. Becca swallowed, hard.

"It's Larissa," Theo said, as if he couldn't believe what he was saying himself. As if he was testing the words, examining them. "She just woke up."

CHAPTER THIRTEEN

LARISSA'S ROOM WAS buzzing with voices. Becca could see various medical personnel swarming around her bed, poking and prodding and asking questions, while in the small sitting room, Bradford and Helen sat, silent and watchful—and then openly horrified at the sight of Becca walking in with Theo.

"Good God!" Bradford cried, his face twisting. "Why on earth would you bring this creature *here?* And at such a time?"

That was when it hit Becca—forcefully—how ghoulish it was to be the person dressed up like the woman who'd been expected to die just as everyone was coming to terms with the fact she wasn't going to die after all.

Because that hadn't been what she'd been concentrating on during the car ride across town from the West Village. She and Theo had sat in a taut, simmering silence. She'd had no idea what he might have been thinking, and had been afraid to ask. Meanwhile, her head had spun around and around and around. What did this mean? *You know what it means,* her practical inner voice had shot back at her. *You just don't want to believe it.*

She'd been aware that she should be worried about what this meant for Emily's future—if she would still get that impossibly large sum of money now, since it wasn't her fault she'd been unable to complete her part of the contract. But she couldn't worry about that. Not then. Not when her whole being seemed to be stuck on a precipice, tottering in the wind, and all too aware that she was about to tumble—because all she wanted to know was what this meant for Theo. For Theo, and for Becca herself. For, God help her, the both of them.

If Larissa was awake, that meant Theo was still engaged to her. And that made everything that had happened between them sordid and wrong. She'd felt her stomach twist as the thoughts raced through her brain. It had been one thing when Larissa was for all intents and purposes already dead. But this…

Becca wasn't the kind of woman who could merrily jump into bed with a committed man. The very thought made her stomach turn. And yet, sitting there in that car, she'd reached the inescapable conclusion that she'd become that kind of woman, despite her best intentions, along with everything else she'd become in this place. With these people. How could she consider them corrupt when she was clearly no better?

"I don't understand what happened," Theo said, his rough tone snapping Becca back to the present, where both Whitneys gaped at her as if she'd thrown something in their faces. "How is this possible?"

"It's a miracle," Helen said at once, piously, holding her hands in her lap as if she expected the queen to happen by and comment on her posture. "You can't call it anything else."

"I don't care what you call it," Bradford snapped. He eyed Becca with what she could only describe as loathing. It crawled over her skin, making goose bumps rise up even as her stomach twisted yet again. He waved a hand at Becca. "It means that we can get rid of this mess, and handle things the proper way. The way they should have been handled from the start, without involving outsiders."

"You're good at getting rid of messes, aren't you?" Becca asked him, not knowing she meant to speak—but not doing anything to curtail it, either. "Poor Larissa. She thought she was escaping, and instead she has to wake up and suffer through more of your brand of parenting. She's the one mess you can't get rid of, isn't she?"

"You're nothing but trash," Bradford said softly, and his face took on that faux-kindly glow that made him so monstrous, so horrifying. "Trash with my daughter's face."

"Watch yourself," Theo advised him, but Bradford did not so much as look at him, rising to his feet and moving closer to Becca, presumably so she could comprehend fully the whole of his contempt as he glared at her. She glared back, unmoved.

"If it had been up to me, you never would have darkened the door of this house again," Bradford told her in that same quietly horrible voice. "Nothing gives me greater pleasure than to send you packing without a single cent of the Whitney fortune. Neither you nor your low-class sister deserve a penny of it. Just like your tramp of a mother before you."

There was, Becca discovered in that moment, a certain liberty in having lost everything—even those things she hadn't known she could lose in the first place, like her heart. It made her entirely immune to bullies like this man.

"I used to think my mother was the victim here," she told Bradford, meeting his glare with her own, not in the least bit afraid of him. "But I understand now that she was lucky to escape this place."

"Yes," Bradford sneered. "Lucky to live in poverty, passed from one inappropriate man to the next. Lucky to raise up two brats while working herself half to death. Yes, Caroline was *lucky*." He laughed. "And you can look forward to being just as lucky, for the rest of your life."

"Bradford." Theo's voice was all steel, all command. "Stop." But still, the other man gave no sign of hearing him. Or perhaps he simply didn't care. Neither did she.

"The truth is that I pity you," Becca told him, leaning in just a little bit, looking him straight in the eye. "You have everything in the world—more than most people could possibly dream of having—and in the end you still have nothing."

"Enough." Becca hadn't even heard Theo move, but then his hands came down on her shoulders and she could *feel* the way he looked at Bradford from behind her. "This is hardly the time for this kind of display," he snapped.

"Get that creature out of my house," Bradford hissed back, furious.

Theo moved so he was between Becca and Bradford, and Becca appreciated the implied chivalry of it even if she would have preferred to continue sniping at Bradford up close. It was much too satisfying—no doubt indicative of yet another character flaw. But it was far better to fight with a toad like Bradford than to think about everything she'd lost tonight. Far better to pretend she was bulletproof and everything just bounced right off her.

Theo moved again, nearer to Bradford, and it brought

her closer to Larissa's door. She couldn't help glancing over. The sea of doctors parted, and for a long moment, a heartbeat and then another, Becca locked eyes with the real Larissa. They stared at each other until the doctors closed in again, and Becca turned away.

It shook her to the bone.

These were real people, she reminded herself, not puppets in some ancient feud. *People*—and one of those people was that poor woman on the bed in there, who deserved more than this depressing little show just inches from where she'd become a medical miracle. It was time for Becca to remember who she'd been back when she was real. It was time to go.

"You don't have to tell me twice," she told Bradford. She even smiled. "I'm happy to be rid of you, once and for all." She raised her brows at him, challenging him. Daring him to insult her further, to push her one more time. "And the next time you need a doppelgänger for one of your Byzantine little plots, I'm busy."

Bradford began to speak, but some swift motion by Theo cut him off. Becca let her gaze sweep over Helen, who stared back at her, all haughty affront, and she told herself it was just as well. She knew how to handle rejection. She knew how to roll with the same old punches she'd been dodging her whole life. If she wished that Helen had been as across-the-board repulsive as Bradford had, well, that was only because she was still so weak somewhere deep inside, where she would always be that not-good-enough girl. Where she wondered sometimes if she would ever feel anything but illegitimate. Helen's small moment of near kindness hurt far more than any of Bradford's tirades.

But she would lock that away, too. With everything else she now had to forget.

She didn't bother looking at Bradford again, and she didn't dare to so much as glance at Theo. Not directly. If she did, she suspected she would never leave, and he was not hers. He had never been hers. She should never have let herself imagine that he could be.

So she simply walked out the door.

Theo caught up with her again where he had once long ago, in the great entryway. When Becca had been someone else. She hardly remembered who.

"Stop," he said, his voice ringing out, ringing in her, making her stop in her tracks just as she had so long before. Just as she always would, she suspected. "Please," he added, and she wondered that he even knew the word.

"There is no point in further, unpleasant conversations," she said. She could feel him as he closed the space between them, coming up behind her. She could sense the heat of him, the height and the power. Her eyes drifted closed—but she snapped them back open. This was no time for dreams about what could have been. It was long past time for reality.

"Bradford is an ass," Theo said darkly. He moved around to face her, and it hurt her to see the set of his jaw, the tense way he held himself. "Obviously, you'll receive the money you would have collected had you met with Van Housen tonight, as planned. No one could have foreseen…this."

"'Met' with him," she murmured, trying to sound arch, amused. Yet she could barely manage anything much beyond shell-shocked. "That sounds so… sanitized."

"I don't think I could have let you go through with it," he said, his gaze searching hers, his tone urgent. "When it came right down to it, I don't think I could have borne it."

She shook her head at him. There were so many things she could have said, that she wanted to say, but she couldn't allow herself such luxuries. She would only regret them later.

"We'll never know," she said, with a shrug. His mouth tightened, and his eyes grew hard. He looked away— as if he fought for control—and when he met her gaze again he was cold, in control.

She hated it.

"You executed your part of the contract flawlessly," he said, every inch the dispassionate CEO. "Of course you will receive what you were promised, no matter what tantrums Bradford throws."

"I don't care!" she threw at him, slashing her hand in the air—but he reached out and caught it in his. The sudden contact startled her into silence. It was too much. Too hot. Too right. Too…all the things it was not, all the things it could not ever be.

"You will." His voice was so low. Too low. It made her…wish for things she couldn't let herself want. "Perhaps not now. But you will."

She pulled her hand from his, feeling a strange heat move through her, knowing she flushed bright with it but not able to stop it. Just as she was unable to push past him and walk away, as she knew she should.

The moment seemed to grow, to echo, to consume them both. There was nothing in the world but his fierce, beloved face, and those arresting, impossibly amber eyes. There was nothing but the things they could not say, spinning between them, louder and louder with each breath.

"I know I should not ask this…" he began, as if the words hurt him.

"Then do not ask it," she replied, firmly, desperately, though there was more of her than she wanted to admit that wanted him to ask it anyway. Whatever it was. Because if he asked, how could she resist? How would she be able to tear herself away? It was killing her already and she hadn't even gone yet.

He whispered her name, and her heart—so broken already, so battered—crumbled into dust.

But she could see herself in the great mirror that graced the near wall, and she did not even look like herself. She looked like Larissa, and the real Larissa was awake—which meant that Becca had no idea, anymore, who she was. How could she? She'd gotten lost in this maze of a life, all mirrors and reflections and charades, for far too long. She had started to believe she belonged here. She had even started to *want* to belong here.

And because she loved this man, she had been prepared to walk into that club and perform whatever act was necessary to make him happy. She would have to live with that truth, with what that said about her and about what parts of herself she was willing to sacrifice for no very good reason. But she didn't have to compound the error.

She'd been settling for less her whole life, and calling it a victory. She couldn't do that any longer. She wouldn't. Not when she'd let herself imagine how it would be if she wasn't the secondhand girl, the throwaway girl. Not when she'd felt what it might be like to be the one finally chosen. It might have been an illusion, but it had changed her. For good.

And much as she wanted to be close to him, no matter

what, she couldn't go back from that. She couldn't un-know it. Which meant that for once in her life, she couldn't allow herself to settle. Not even if that meant keeping him somehow.

"I deserve more than the scraps from the Whitney family's table," she said, surprised to hear that her voice was clear. Even proud. No matter how much she shook inside. "I deserve more than to wonder who you really see when you look at me—or who you want to see." She heard his muttered oath, but continued. "I deserve more than the little you have to give, the little that isn't focused on what you really love."

"I don't love her." His voice was stark. Sure.

"I was going to say power." She could not let herself react to what he'd said. She could not let it matter. "Money. Wealth. All those things you dreamed of back in Miami." She searched his face. "I understand it, but I deserve more, Theo. I deserve better."

"Becca." He looked so lost that it made her waver for a moment.

One last time, she forced herself to be strong—stronger than she should ever have had to be. She leaned in close, letting his scent tease at her, and she pressed a single kiss to his lean, hard jaw. And then, somehow, she pulled away.

"Please," he whispered fiercely, his hands in fists at his side, his big body rigid and almost quivering with tension.

"Goodbye, Theo," she whispered back, her throat tight with the tears she fought to keep at bay.

And then she walked away from him, from the only man she'd ever loved, toward whatever future awaited her without him. But at least, this once, she hadn't settled for what she could get. It had to be better to hold out for what she really wanted—for what she deserved.

It just had to be.

It was two days, perhaps three—he'd long since lost track of time—when Theo finally found himself the single visitor in Larissa's room. No doctors. No hovering Whitneys. Just him and the woman he was still engaged to marry. The woman he'd written off as dead, who as far as he was concerned had come back to life from the grave.

He hardly knew how to feel about that. Not that he could feel much of anything. He'd been numb ever since Becca had walked away from him, letting the grand door of the Whitney mansion slam shut behind her, severing whatever had been between them. *Numb.* He supposed that was better than what lurked beneath it.

And now he was the man who sat at the bedside of his convalescent fiancée, thinking of another woman.

So far from the man he'd thought he'd be, he reflected darkly, with no little self-loathing. So very far from the man he should have been.

She stirred, and woke, and Theo was still surprised that she was not Becca. That she was nothing like Becca at all. How had he convinced himself that they were similar? It wasn't just that Larissa was so pale, so fragile-looking. It was that the whole bright thrust of Becca's personality simply…wasn't there. It was like looking at a black-and-white photograph when he'd grown so used to color.

"Am I hallucinating?" Larissa asked, her voice raspy, as if from a rough night in a bar. Theo wondered that his mind went there, directly, when he knew perfectly well it was from the tubes that had kept her alive. Or perhaps he shouldn't wonder. She'd been in one of those bars before her collapse, hadn't she? It would behoove him to remember that she was still Larissa, no matter how small and wan she looked today.

"I can't imagine why you would hallucinate me," he said. She smiled, and he saw the Larissa he'd liked the most peek out of her eyes for a moment. The Larissa he'd fantasized would be the one he'd marry, because he'd thought that was the real Larissa. The one she kept so deep inside, so locked away, that he doubted many people saw glimpses of her at all.

"Out there," she said, nodding toward the outer room. She frowned in confusion. "I thought…I thought I saw…"

"You weren't hallucinating," he said quietly.

She looked at him for a long moment, her green eyes serious—very nearly contemplative—and all he could think was that she was a stranger to him. That he had known her for years and he'd never known her at all. He did not elaborate further, and she did not ask.

"Thank you," she said. "You've always been honest with me."

That pricked at his conscience, though he knew she could not mean it to do so.

She sat up slowly, awkwardly, but she waved him away when he moved to help, and eventually she propped herself up against her pillows, her breath coming hard. He should feel more, he thought, despairing of himself. He should feel more for her than pity.

"You should rest," he said. "You'll need all your strength to recover."

"I forgot about the will," she said, and coughed a little bit. "My father reminded me." She sighed, and looked at her hands, and Theo had no trouble imagining how unpleasant that conversation must have been.

"Don't worry about your father," he said.

"I'm sorry." She shook her head. "It's not that I wanted to hurt you. I just wanted to make him…something. Anything. I don't know."

"We don't have to talk about this," Theo said gruffly. He could not remember the last time Larissa had spoken to him like this. No games, no ulterior motives. No tests. There was a time when it would have changed his whole world, when it would have filled him with hope and joy. It would have meant that he'd finally gotten precisely where he'd always wanted to go.

So why did he feel so empty? But he knew.

"We do," she said. She pushed her pale hair back from her face, showing her high cheekbones that made him wish she was Becca, her mouth that was not quite Becca's. And when she spoke, it was with her voice that was not Becca's at all. "I'll change the will. I'll sign it all over to you." She took a quick breath. "And I'll marry you. I won't…" She floundered for a moment, then her shoulders sank, and her face cleared of all expression. "I won't resist anymore." She looked at him then, her gaze more sad than anything else. "I promise."

He should have been jubilant. He should have felt some hint of triumph, of victory. Because he believed her. Whatever she'd just been through had changed her somehow, at least so far—and he could see it. He believed it. Which meant that she'd just offered him everything he'd ever wanted on a silver platter. It was his for the taking.

But *everything he'd ever wanted* didn't mean the same things to him that it had once.

"Keep your shares," he said. Her eyes flew to his.

"But—"

"Keep them," he said. "They're your birthright."

"I don't care about my birthright," she told him. "I really don't."

"But it's yours just the same," he said gently. "And maybe someday you'll think that the least you deserve for all the trouble of surviving this family is a stake in it all. You never know."

She studied him for a moment, but did not speak. Theo climbed to his feet, and rubbed his hands over his face. He couldn't remember the last time he'd shaved. There had been too much going on the past few days. Bradford had told him he looked like a *ruffian,* and he'd taken it as a compliment when once he might have worried that he'd let his poverty-stricken roots show through. His true face, poor and desperate and nothing but ambitious. But he no longer cared.

He cared about one thing, in all this great mess, and he'd let her walk away from him.

"I owe you an apology," he told Larissa.

"I doubt that," she said. But her eyes were solemn on his, as if she thought something else entirely. He had a moment of regret, for all the mysteries he would never uncover about this woman, who seemed to be so very altered today, with none of her usual masks. But it was gone so quickly, he almost thought he'd imagined it.

"I think I loved what I wanted you to be," he said, testing out the words, feeling the truth of them roar through him, making sense of all the past years. "Not you. Never you."

There was something so weary in her gaze then, something sad and wise, and he wondered if this, right now when it had ceased to matter, was the real Larissa he'd been searching for all these years. She gazed at him for a long moment, and then her mouth crooked into a wry sort of smile.

"I know," she said simply.

And set them both free.

CHAPTER FOURTEEN

WHEN HER COWORKER popped her head into Becca's office and told her, in a hushed tone of deepest awe, that she had a *male visitor,* Becca felt as if all the blood drained out of her head. She took a breath, then another. Only when she was reasonably sure that she wouldn't topple over in a faint did she manage to smile.

"Please have him wait for me in Reception," she said, as calmly as possible. "I'll be out when I can."

"I don't think this is the kind of man who waits," Amy said, starry-eyed, still in that *amazed* sort of tone. Becca only smiled.

But when Amy disappeared again, she felt her smile slip from her face. She reached up and rubbed at her temples, closing her eyes for a moment against the swell of emotion that threatened to tip her over in her chair.

He was here.

She had no doubt at all that it was Theo. She couldn't think of another man alive who would render the usually sophisticated Amy so flabbergasted. He had that effect.

It had been two weeks since she'd walked out of the Whitney mansion. She'd congratulated herself. She'd told herself that she'd accomplished all she'd set out to accomplish. She'd walked into the belly of the beast and came out the other side, as planned. Surely that had to matter. The simple *fact* of her survival.

She'd come home to Boston, immediately had her hair dyed back to its natural color as a clear gesture toward reclaiming her old self, and picked up her life right where she'd left off. It had been wonderful to see her sister again—and to see the acceptance letters Emily had received from every single college she'd applied to, making what Becca had gone through worthwhile, after all.

"I know we can't afford it," Emily had said, holding the letter from Princeton in her hand, but her eyes had shone so brightly, so proudly, anyway. "But I wanted to see if I could do it at all."

"Don't worry about the money," Becca had said, hugging her. "That's my job."

It didn't matter what had happened to her in New York, Becca had thought then. She'd still believed that Theo would give her that money, as he'd said he would, and that meant everything had been worth it. Everything. Even her broken heart. If it meant Emily could have the future she deserved—and that Becca could finally make it up to her poor mother as she'd promised to do—then she would have done it all over again.

She might have had to beg a little bit to walk right back into her job, but they'd eventually relented—even if, as punishment, she'd gotten assigned to the crankiest, most demanding lawyer in the firm. She could handle that.

What she was not at all sure she could handle was an infusion of Theo into her neat, orderly little life. It was one thing to live in his Manhattan dream-life. Penthouses and private cars and the best of everything laid out for his pleasure. But this was *her* life, and he was too big. Too overpowering. *Too much*. He didn't belong here. Not even for as long as it took him to do whatever errand he'd planned to do on this unexpected visit of his.

But she was going to have to dredge up the strength to tell him that, and Becca wasn't sure she could do it. Not when she'd done nothing but ache for him, wide-awake and hollow-eyed, every sleepless night, since she'd left New York.

So she did the only thing she could do. She made him wait.

How long would she make him wait? Theo stretched out his long legs and ignored the receptionist's blatant stare. It was coming up on an hour, and yet he still sat, in the small little office that housed this second-rate law firm she worked for. It was not the sort of place he would ordinarily grace with his presence, but then, what about Becca had ever been ordinary?

He knew the moment she entered the reception area, though she did it from the side door and he could only sense her out of his peripheral vision at first. Still, he knew at once it was her. His Becca. He would know her if he was blind.

"Almost an hour you've let me sit here," he said, still pretending to flip through the magazine he'd picked up when brooding at the carpet had bored him. "Is that sufficient penance for you?"

"Not even close," she said, her voice crisp.

He looked up then, letting his eyes drink her in. Two weeks without her had felt like a lifetime. He had no intention of repeating the experience. She'd darkened her hair, and rid herself of those damned green contacts.

He liked it. There was something about the chestnut color of her hair, swept back into a competent bun today, that worked with her mossy-hazel eyes, and the less she looked like Larissa, the more he liked it.

How had he ever considered her dowdy? Because he knew he had, though he could not seem to access those memories. He got too caught on the images of the two of them naked, Becca moaning out his name, while he moved hard and deep inside of her.

She was wearing what he supposed passed for a business suit. It was nice enough, though it only hinted at her delectable body beneath. He knew that was undoubtedly more professional, but he preferred her in more revealing clothes.

"Hello, Becca," he said after a long moment, when they only stared at each other.

Her face colored with temper, and her eyes crackled. She shot a look over her shoulder at the receptionist who wasn't even attempting to hide her avid interest, and then jerked her head toward the door.

"Come on," she said, her voice clipped. It was a direct order and despite himself, he found it delightful. "Let's go for a walk."

He put the magazine aside and stood, slowly, watching her. A very male satisfaction flashed through him when he saw the way her eyes tracked the movement of his body, the way she swallowed, hard. *Good,* he thought. As long as she still wanted him, he could handle the rest. That was the only part that mattered.

She jerked her gaze away from his abdomen and met his gaze, and he could see the flush on her cheeks was as much desire as temper now. She might hate him. In fact, she should. But that didn't mean she wanted him any less.

Far happier than he should have been, he followed her outside.

She whirled on him the moment they hit the sidewalk, the midday buzz of downtown Boston disappearing as she focused on him.

"'Hello, Becca?'" she echoed, in disbelief. "Is that really what you said to me? As if we are nothing but casual acquaintances?"

"Is there some other way you would like me to greet you?" he asked in that lazy way that made her suspect he was laughing at her. And it hurt too much. She was too raw and he shouldn't be here—he was too powerful a presence, even in nothing more than a dark sweater, a coat and jeans. He was attracting stares from all the passing alpha male lawyers on their way to meetings, depositions and court appearances, because he was something different, something more, than all of them. He lit up the Boston street like a supernova.

Though Theo, of course, noticed none of that. He only watched her as if she was prey. Or something precious to him. Or both. She could not decide which was worse, which would damage her more completely.

"What do you want?" she asked woodenly.

He pulled a thick envelope from the inside pocket of his coat and handed it to her. She took it without meaning to, and stared at it in her hand.

"What is this?" She felt dull. Thick. She wanted him to go away. Or in any case, that was what she *should* want.

"What do you think?" His amber eyes saw too much. They touched too many places inside of her she would prefer to keep hidden. "It is your money. There are some forms to sign, and some investment portfolios you should consider with an inheritance of this size, and, of course, tax issues." His brows rose. "I'm happy to recommend a good lawyer if you would prefer the ones you work for not know your new net worth. It may be better to keep such things private."

She couldn't take it in. That he was here, or that she was holding an entirely different life in her hands, the culmination of her wildest dreams tucked into this little envelope.

"Have you become a messenger boy in your spare time?" she managed to ask, concentrating on the one thing—the only thing—that she could make herself focus on. "You deliver the mail?"

"Only to you, Becca," he said, his voice so rich, so deep, that it seemed to inhabit her, taking her over and making her melt. How could he have this power over her?

But even as despair washed through her, it was met with desire, stronger and hotter and far more dangerous. As if he could sense it, or read it on her skin like text, he reached over and cupped her face with his warm, strong palm.

She had to fight against the urge to turn her face into his hand. Tears pricked the back of her eyes, and this was all too unfair.

"Why are you doing this to me?" she whispered. "Is this a game? Do you want to be the one to walk away this time, so you can keep up your winning streak? Is that what you came for?"

She thought he would drop his hand, but he only moved it, sliding it down her neck to rest against her collarbone, where she had no doubt he could feel the wild fluttering of her pulse.

"I love—" he began, but panic soared in her, thick and smoky and desperate.

"Your power games," she interrupted him. "Your boardrooms and your corporate suits and however else you plan to rule the world. I know what you love."

"Becca." His voice was a command. A strict order. But this time, she could not allow herself to obey it. There was too much at stake—and she had already lost more than she could bear.

"Women who do not exist—figments of your imagination," she continued, breathless and chaotic, not even knowing what she meant to say. "The whole corrupt and despicable Whitney family, who would cast you aside in a heartbeat if you did not contribute to their ever-swelling coffers. That's what you love. Greed and snobbery. Fantasies and—"

"And you," he said. His gaze was serious, and her heart stuttered in her chest. "I love you."

A fierce joy slammed into her, so hard it took her breath away, but then sanity returned and with it, another wave of that crippling despair. It didn't matter what she wanted, because she knew him. She knew him too well, and while she loved him with a ferocity that shocked her on some level, she had walked away from him for a reason.

"No, you don't," she said, her voice small but sure. "Not enough."

She stepped back from him before his hand on her drove her to distraction. Before he made her forget herself, and the sad truth of things.

"What would prove it to you?" he asked, almost idly, as if he was not particularly concerned. But she could see the fire in his gaze. The steely determination. It made her shiver slightly. "Because I already know that you love me, though you have never bothered to say it." His hard mouth crooked into a smile. "I can see it even now."

"Why would I tell you something like that?" she asked, and realized as she did that she hadn't denied it. She couldn't. "And what does it matter anyway? You're engaged. Everything that happened between us is wrong."

"I am not engaged," he countered. "And what happened between us was many things, Becca, but none of it was wrong!"

"But…" She wanted so badly for what he was saying to be true that she was afraid that she was making it up in her own head. "What happened to Larissa?"

His amber eyes burned as he looked at her, but his voice was soft when he spoke.

"She's fine," he said. "She offered to make good on all of her promises." His gaze was like steel. Serious. Sure. "I declined."

"You…" She couldn't make sense of it. Her heart was pounding too hard, too fast. She felt slightly dizzy, slightly ill. But she couldn't look away from him.

"I left her shares in her possession," he said, very deliberately, moving close again. "I won't be marrying her."

"But Whitney Media is your whole life!" she managed to say, though she felt as if she stood on shaking ground, as if the earth rocked beneath her, as if the slightest breeze would fling her sideways and she was not sure she would ever get up again.

"About that," he said. Dark humor lit his eyes, and she could not help but be drawn to it. To him. Even now, even knowing that she should turn and run in the opposite direction. "I quit."

She felt her mouth drop open. She felt that shuddering again, from deep inside, that threatened to break her into pieces.

And then she couldn't seem to keep herself together anymore. It was all too much. Becca stared at him for another moment, fighting a losing battle, and then could do nothing but burst into tears.

"I don't understand any of this," Becca said a long time later, standing in Theo's massive hotel suite that looked out over the city of Boston as the sun began to inch toward the horizon.

He had taken care of everything. He had bundled her sobbing form into his waiting limousine, contacted her employers and then whisked her off to one of Boston's most outrageously expensive hotels to let her cry it out in peace. He even held her while she did so, his warm hand against her back, his soothing murmur in her ear.

And oh, how she had cried. She'd cried for her poor mother, and for the tiny little baby she'd been when she'd been treated like nothing more than a bomb in her mother's life. She'd cried for her guilt ever after, for the life she'd kept her mother from, and for the life they'd led together, traipsing from one bad male figure to the next. She'd cried for the promises she'd made and the faith that she'd broken with herself to even dare to ask the Whitneys for help in the first place. She'd cried for Emily's innocence and her own loss of it, but most of all, she'd simply cried to get out all of the shattering emotions that had wrecked her, again and again, since the day she'd met this man.

And when the storm was over, when it had wrung her dry at last, he had still been there.

"What don't you understand?" he asked now. He stood by the window, where she'd found him when she'd emerged from the long, hot shower she'd felt she had to take after such an extended crying jag. Now she was dressed in nothing more than a thick robe, her hair scraped back, her face free of any cosmetics, and on some intellectual level she imagined this should make her feel vulnerable, this near nudity. But she could not imagine feeling any more stripped than she already did, simply by being in his presence. So what could what she wore matter?

"You worked too hard at Whitney Media," she said. "*For* Whitney Media." He turned to look at her, and her breath caught as it always did, because he was far too beautiful, far too dangerous. And his eyes glittered like jewels. She faltered for a moment, but then blinked and remembered herself. "Why would you give that up now? When it could have finally been yours the way you wanted it?"

He stood there, big and dark against the window, and he made her legs feel weak, her breasts feel full. And in the core of her, as ever, she melted.

"Simple," he said. "I want you more."

How could she keep shattering? When there could be nothing left to break into pieces?

"No one chooses me," she said, her voice a thick, uneven rasp. "I'm the second best, the fill-in. And you… you're the kind of man who would never be satisfied with anything but the real thing."

"The real you, Becca," he said, moving toward her. "I want the real you."

"But you can't." She couldn't get her head around it. She couldn't let herself believe it. "You can't."

"I do," he said, and then he lifted her into his arms, and pressed his mouth to hers.

The heat of it exploded through her. Fire and fury, and all of it ripe with joy. A terrible, impossible joy—but she found that now that she was in his arms again, she couldn't seem to fight it. She could only taste him, again and again, and it was not enough. It was never enough.

She pulled away to peer up into his face, and what she saw there made her tremble. So much need. So much fire. And beyond that, the love. Fierce and uncompromising, and this time, she had no doubt at all that it was really her he wanted, and not the woman she happened to resemble.

Because he'd had that woman, and he'd let her go. And now he was here. With Becca, not with the object of all his fantasies across the years. Even she couldn't manage to make that less than it was.

And so slowly, carefully, Becca began to let herself believe. To hope where she had previously only doubted. It felt like sunlight, creeping in through the smallest of cracks, changing her from within.

"I am unemployed and no doubt blacklisted by one of the most powerful companies in the world," he said, settling his hands at her shoulders, pulling her even closer to him, so that her breasts met the hard wall of his chest. "This is how I've come to tell you that I love you, that I want to marry you, that there can be no other ending to this story."

She let the dizziness move through her, as she processed words that she'd never let herself hope to hear from him, and then she smiled, and she felt it all the way to her toes.

"Too bad I'm now a Whitney heiress," she said. "It does rather take away from your great sacrifice."

"I love you," he said again, more seriously. "It's all hollow and pointless without you."

"I know," she whispered, tears falling once again, wetting her cheeks, but this time, from too much joy. Too much hope. She let them fall unchecked. "I love you, too."

Much later, they lay naked and entwined in the wide hotel bed, just as he preferred them to be, still basking in the glow of their reunion. With each touch, each kiss, Theo could see the way she changed. Hope. Belief. Love. She was wary, he thought, but she was his. And he was a very patient man when he chose to be.

And with Becca, he could be the man he'd meant to be all along. With Becca, he could finally be himself.

"You walked away from a fortune," she said, tracing idle patterns on his chest and smiling. "For me."

"I did," he said. He had never felt this completeness, this certainty. He had never loved before. He was not sure he'd even wanted to, and so he'd chosen a fantasy instead. But now… Now he had the rest of his life to love this woman, and to be worthy of her love in return. All of it undeniably real. He grinned down at her. "But never fear, my love. I am Theo Markou Garcia. I'll make another fortune. It's what I do."

* * * * *

CLASSIC

Harlequin *Presents*

COMING NEXT MONTH from Harlequin Presents®
AVAILABLE JUNE 26, 2012

#3071 HEART OF A DESERT WARRIOR
Lucy Monroe
Sheikh Asad needs to secure his legacy, and Iris is the key.
Can she resist so determined a seduction?

#3072 SANTINA'S SCANDALOUS PRINCESS
The Santina Crown
Kate Hewitt
Pampered princess Natalia has swapped couture and
cocktails for photocopying! How long will she last working
for the devilishly handsome Ben Jackson?

#3073 DEFYING DRAKON
The Lyonedes Legacy
Carole Mortimer
Drakon Lyonedes has power, wealth, sex appeal...and any
woman he wants! Until beautiful Gemini Bartholomew enters
his life, that is...

#3074 CAPTIVE BUT FORBIDDEN
Lynn Raye Harris
Bodyguard Rajesh Vala must protect Veronica—whatever the
cost.... But Veronica has always rebelled against commands
and isn't making Raj's job easy!

#3075 HIS MAJESTY'S MISTAKE
A Royal Scandal
Jane Porter
Princess Emmeline is everything this desert king shouldn't
want... Posing as her twin sister and Makin's secretary, she's
playing with fire!

#3076 THE DARK SIDE OF DESIRE
Julia James
Business legend Leon Marantz exudes a dark power that
sends shivers through Flavia Lassiter's body—threatening to
shatter the icy shell protecting her heart.

You can find more information on upcoming Harlequin®
titles, free excerpts and more at www.Harlequin.com.

HPCNM0612

REQUEST YOUR FREE BOOKS!

Harlequin *Presents*®

2 FREE NOVELS PLUS
2 FREE GIFTS!

PASSION GUARANTEED SEDUCTION

YES! Please send me 2 FREE Harlequin Presents® novels and my 2 FREE gifts (gifts are worth about $10). After receiving them, if I don't wish to receive any more books, I can return the shipping statement marked "cancel." If I don't cancel, I will receive 6 brand-new novels every month and be billed just $4.30 per book in the U.S. or $4.99 per book in Canada. That's a saving of at least 14% off the cover price! It's quite a bargain! Shipping and handling is just 50¢ per book in the U.S. and 75¢ per book in Canada.* I understand that accepting the 2 free books and gifts places me under no obligation to buy anything. I can always return a shipment and cancel at any time. Even if I never buy another book, the two free books and gifts are mine to keep forever.

106/306 HDN FERQ

Name _____ (PLEASE PRINT) _____

Address _____ Apt. # _____

City _____ State/Prov. _____ Zip/Postal Code _____

Signature (if under 18, a parent or guardian must sign)

Mail to the **Reader Service:**
IN U.S.A.: P.O. Box 1867, Buffalo, NY 14240-1867
IN CANADA: P.O. Box 609, Fort Erie, Ontario L2A 5X3

Not valid for current subscribers to Harlequin Presents books.

**Are you a current subscriber to Harlequin Presents books
and want to receive the larger-print edition?
Call 1-800-873-8635 or visit www.ReaderService.com.**

* Terms and prices subject to change without notice. Prices do not include applicable taxes. Sales tax applicable in N.Y. Canadian residents will be charged applicable taxes. Offer not valid in Quebec. This offer is limited to one order per household. All orders subject to credit approval. Credit or debit balances in a customer's account(s) may be offset by any other outstanding balance owed by or to the customer. Please allow 4 to 6 weeks for delivery. Offer available while quantities last.

Your Privacy—The Reader Service is committed to protecting your privacy. Our Privacy Policy is available online at www.ReaderService.com or upon request from the Reader Service.

We make a portion of our mailing list available to reputable third parties that offer products we believe may interest you. If you prefer that we not exchange your name with third parties, or if you wish to clarify or modify your communication preferences, please visit us at www.ReaderService.com/consumerschoice or write to us at Reader Service Preference Service, P.O. Box 9062, Buffalo, NY 14269. Include your complete name and address.

HPI1B

*Patricia Thayer welcomes you to Larkville, Texas,
in THE COWBOY COMES HOME—book 1 in the exciting
new 8-book miniseries,* THE LARKVILLE LEGACY,
from Harlequin® Romance.

REACHING THE BANK, Jess climbed down, smiling as she walked her mount to the water. "Wow, I haven't ridden like that in years."

"You're good."

"I'm Clay Calhoun's daughter. I'm supposed to be a good rider."

"You miss him."

She walked with him through the stiff winter grass to the tree. "It's hard to imagine the Double Bar C going on without him. He loved this land." She glanced around the landscape. "Now my brother runs the operation, but he'll be gone awhile." She released a breath. "I have to say we miss his leadership."

He frowned. "Is there anything I can do?"

"Thank you. You're handling Storm—that's a big enough help. It's just that it would be nice to have my brothers and sister here." She looked at him. "Do you have any siblings?"

He shook his head. "None that I know of."

"What about your father?" she asked.

He shook his head. "Never been in my life. I tried for years to track him down, but I never could catch up with him."

He caught the sadness etched on her face. "Johnny, I'm sorry."

He hated pity, especially from her. "Why? You had nothing to do with it. Jake Jameson didn't want to be found, or meet his son." He shrugged. "You can't miss what you've never had. I'm not much of a homebody, either. I guess that's why I like to keep moving."

Jess looked out over the land. "I guess that's where we're different. I've never really moved away from Larkville."

"Why should you want to leave? You have your business here and your home."

She smiled. "I had to fight Dad to live on my own. But I've got a little Calhoun stubbornness, too."

"You got all the beauty."

Johnny came closer, removed her hat and studied her face. "Your eyes are incredible. And your mouth… I could kiss you for hours."

She sucked in a breath and raised her gaze to his. "Johnny… We weren't going to start this."

"Don't look now, darlin', but it's already started."

Find out what happens between Johnny and Jess in
THE COWBOY COMES HOME by Patricia Thayer,
available July 2012!

And find out how Jess's family will be transformed
in the 8-book series:
THE LARKVILLE LEGACY
A secret letter…two families changed forever

This summer, celebrate everything Western
with Harlequin® Books!

www.Harlequin.com/Western

Harlequin Romance

The LARKVILLE LEGACY

A secret letter…two families changed forever

Welcome to Larkville, Texas, where the Calhoun family has
been ranching for generations. When Jess Calhoun discovers
a secret, unopened letter written to her late father, she learns
that there is a whole other branch of her family. Find out
what happens when the two sides meet….

**A new Larkville Legacy story is available every
month beginning July 2012.**

Collect all 8 tales!

Harlequin *Romance*

Three billionaire brothers. Three guarded hearts.
Three fabulous stories.

SHIRLEY JUMP

begins a new miniseries that is sure
to capture your heart.

When self-made millionaire and CEO Finn McKenna finds his
business in trouble due to a very public scandal, he turns to business
rival Ellie Winston for help. But Ellie wants a different kind
of merger—marriage!

ONE DAY TO FIND A HUSBAND
Available in July

And coming soon!

HOW THE PLAYBOY GOT SERIOUS
Riley McKenna's story, available in August

THE RETURN OF THE LAST McKENNA
Brody McKenna's story, available in September

Available wherever books are sold.

SPECIAL EDITION

Life, Love and Family

USA TODAY bestselling author

Leanne Banks

begins a heartwarming new miniseries

Royal Babies

When princess Pippa Devereaux learns that the mother of Texas tycoon and longtime business rival Nic Lafitte is terminally ill she secretly goes against her family's wishes and helps Nic fulfill his mother's dying wish. Nic is awed by Pippa's kindness and quickly finds himself falling for her. But can their love break their long-standing family feud?

THE PRINCESS AND THE OUTLAW

Available July 2012!
Wherever books are sold.

HSE65680